Toughing It

Toughing It

by Nancy Springer

HARCOURT
BRACE &
COMPANY

San Diego
New York
London

Library of Congress Cataloging-in-Publication Data
Springer, Nancy.
Toughing It/Nancy Springer.—1st ed.
p.   cm.
Summary: Sixteen-year-old Shawn must deal with his loss and
anger after witnessing his older brother's murder.
ISBN 0-15-200008-9.—ISBN 0-15-200011-9 (pbk.)
[1. Death—Fiction. 2. Murder—Fiction. 3. Brothers—Fiction.]
I. Title
PZ7.S76846To   1994
[Fic]—dc20   93-42231

The text was set in Primer.

Designed by D. W. Blankenship
Printed in Hong Kong
First edition   A B C D E

To Ben

The moment before he died, my brother turned his head to yell something to me above the noise of the dirt bike. He was grinning, teasing me about a girl. "So does she like your stuff, Tuff?" he yelled, and the answer was no, she did not, but I never got to answer. Those were the last words he ever said to me.

It happened like a knife cutting my life in half. We were blasting along the Jeep trail, with me hanging on to his back and his hair whipping me in the face and the trees whacking at both of us as Dillon pushed it faster around a curve—he loved to go fast up that mountain. So did I. He throttled it higher— and there was no warning, no skidding, no sliding, just a flash of light and a boom like thunder and Dillon's head smashing back into mine. The bike flew out from under us. The engine screamed. Maybe I did, too. It's hard to remember. I don't really remember how I fell, or how Dillon and the bike fell, or how I got to my knees in the dirt. All I remember is kneeling there staring down at him.

"Dillon? You all right?"

It was god-awful quiet. The bike had stalled. Dillon stared straight back at me, but his mouth opened without speaking and there was something wrong with the look in his eyes. Then he shuddered all over.

"Dillon!"

Nothing.

"Dillon, goddammit, this is not funny! Get up!"

No answer. It was not a joke. I felt for the pulse at his neck and found blood instead. My hand came away from him sticky with blood. I pulled off my shirt and pressed it against the bloody place, but it was no good—he was not breathing. There was no heartbeat. I got on top of him with my fists on his chest and started shoving, hard, trying to get his heart started, hitting him with everything I had again and again and again. I don't know how long I practically beat on him, trying to make him live, but way back in my mind I already knew it was no use. He was—

No. No, he could not be dead.

"Dillon, please," I whispered.

He did not move or breathe. But he could

not be dead. Probably I was being stupid, not doing the right things for him. I had to get somebody who knew what they were doing, quick. I had to go for help.

I staggered a few steps back down the trail and came face to face with the double barrel of a shotgun staring me down like two hard black eyes. No person, just the gun. I didn't understand what had happened, I was so panicked. Didn't guess it was the murder weapon. I just thought, Who would leave a shotgun there in a tree?

I ran.

It would have been faster to take the bike, but I never thought of it. It was Dillon's. Maybe I didn't feel like I could touch it. I ran all the way to the paved road where there were some trailers strung out between the mountain and the river, and the first one I came to I pounded on the door. A girl opened it, but I was panting so hard I couldn't talk.

"Tuff?" She knew me from somewhere.

I leaned there in her doorway, half bent over with the pain in my chest.

"What happened?" She grabbed a paper napkin and touched my face. It came away soaked with blood. I flinched back, surprised to see all that blood.

"Your nose looks broken," she said. "Did somebody hit you or something?"

I pushed past her and got to the phone. Dialed 911. "My brother," I panted as if there was somebody listening.

"Is he hurt?" the girl asked.

"Dillon. My brother." There was somebody on the emergency line now. "Send an ambulance. He's up on Sid's Mountain, just laying there. Send help."

It was like the knife from hell kept cutting the day into pieces. I must have gone out to stand along the road and wait for the ambulance, but I don't remember doing it, or leading the medics up the mountain. All I remember is being there again, getting back to Dillon, and he hadn't moved at all.

It was—it was scary, the way he looked at me without seeing me. I got to within a few steps of him, and then I had to stop. I could not go closer or touch him. I froze like a deer in headlights, with death coming at me. The medics clustered around Dillon and did their stuff, but in just a couple of minutes they shook their heads and got up. I stood there listening to the cops talking. Three cops, and I don't remember how any of them got there.

4

"Double-O buckshot, looks like," one of them was saying.

I don't remember which one said what or even what they looked like, just what they said.

"Caught him in just the wrong place."

"Set up just the wrong height." The shotgun in the tree, they meant. Trigger's wired back, and then a trip wire going to the hammer, with the end of the wire fastened to a black string stretched across the trail. I figured out how it worked later. Right then I was looking straight at it, yet I did not understand. Not what it was, not what it had done, not what it was meant for, not anything.

"That's the ugliest goddamn thing I ever seen."

"Son." One of them was talking to me. Didn't remember my name, so he called me "son." Wouldn't that be a hoot, if he really was my father? "Son, did you and your brother ride up here often?"

He had to ask me twice before I really heard him and answered.

"Shortest way for him to get to work." My voice came out a whisper.

"So he came through here all the time."

I nodded. Lots of the people who lived along the river used these mountain trails to get to town.

"Do you know who owns this land?"

I shook my head. Probably it was state land, logging company land, mine company land, or something, and what the hell did it matter?

"So you don't have permission to ride here."

I just stared at him. I was numb. Could not believe any of this was happening.

One of the other cops said, "It's still murder, far as I'm concerned."

"Tell that to our wimp D.A. Manslaughter is the most he's likely to go for."

"If we ever get the guy. Damn hard to prove anything. Anybody could have come in here and rigged this up."

"Maybe the detectives will find a footprint or something." He was being sarcastic.

They all laughed. I swear to God, they laughed like it was a show.

Then I must have blipped out again. Next thing I remember, the cops were gone. Dillon's body was gone—where had they taken him? The bike was gone. The shotgun was still there and I was still there, sitting down, with a medic working on my face. "You're lucky you didn't catch any pellets," he said.

I didn't feel lucky.

"Close range," he said. "Buckshot doesn't scatter as much as people think."

I wasn't listening. "Is Dillon dead?" I asked.

The way he nodded made me realize we had been through this before. "You ought to see your doctor in a couple of days," he said, taping up my nose.

Sure. Fat chance. People like us don't have a doctor. "Why is Dillon dead?"

"Shot in the neck," he said. "He probably died within a minute."

That wasn't what I meant. "But why?"

He just sighed and kept putting antiseptic on me. It stung. Good. Life ought to hurt. At least I could feel something.

"I know it doesn't make any sense," the medic said. "At least it was quick." He was a nice guy. For half a second I pretended he could be my father, but nah. Too young.

I did that a lot, pretending some man I met was my father. Dillon and I talked about it sometimes, who the hell our dad might be. Mom would never tell us. We figured we were full brothers because we were only a couple years apart and a lot older than her other kids, but she wouldn't even tell us if we were right about that. Mom was not a bad mom some ways, but some ways she was the pits. Dillon and I would joke about wanting to send her back for repairs. We would joke about dads. When we were little we would play that Dillon was the father because he was older, or we would dream up make-believe dads, all sorts of dads, whatever kind we wanted. But we didn't really need a dad or a mom. We had each other.

Oh, my Christ.

"Dillon's dead," I said to the medic. "Is Dillon dead?"

He said, just as gently as if I didn't already know, "Yes."

All of a sudden I was burning mad. "Who killed him?"

"I don't know."

I swore. No swear word I could think of was bad enough. No name I could think of to call the murderer was bad enough. "The total no-neck slime-faced . . . Who did it?"

The medic said, "You better ask them." He tilted his head toward some men in suits. More cops. These ones were Sherlock Holmes types, nosing around, hunting for cigarette butts and footprints in the weeds, squinting at the way the shotgun was wired up, bossing some guy with a camera and some other guy who was stringing up a lot of yellow tape that said POLICE LINE—DO NOT CROSS. I could see now why the other cops laughed. These detectives were hot dogs. They wouldn't find out anything.

"It shouldn't have happened," I said. "Why did it happen?"

The medic shook his head and went off to find me a ride home.

Our trailer was six miles downstream, set between the road and the water, like all the others along this stretch of river. On the flood plain, where it could get washed out anytime, where nobody with any sense or any choices wanted to live. That's why it was cheap rent. And that's why we were river people. Not much sense, not many choices.

When I got there, the brats were hiding under the trailer, belly-down in the dirt like a bunch of little collie dogs, and the cops were trying to tell Mom what had happened. It was almost suppertime on a Saturday night, so she was drunk and didn't understand them. She thought they were saying her old man was in the slammer again. "I ain't got no money for no bail," she said.

"Mom," I said, "it's Dillon."

She didn't look at me. "You get out of here," she said to the cops. "I didn't do nothing. You just keep him a few days so he don't do nothing to me."

"Ma'am," a cop said, "your boy's dead."

All she did was get mad and wobble a couple steps toward him. "Get the hell out," she said. "You got a warrant? Huh? You don't come in here without no warrant."

The cops didn't care. They had done what they got paid to do, so they just shrugged and left. I grabbed Mom by the shoulders and screamed at her, "Listen to me, goddammit! Dillon is dead!"

She swore and hit me on my sore face for yelling at her. A couple of the kids under the trailer were crying, maybe because they understood what was going on better than she did. Or maybe just because they were hungry. They were my half brothers and sisters, but I never felt all that close to them. Right then I didn't feel anything for them at all, except hate because they were little and allowed to cry.

Not that I would have cried. I got my nickname when I was five years old and tried to pat a snapping turtle practically bigger than I was. It clamped onto my hand like a truck door and broke two of my fingers. Dillon called

Mom, and she had to cut the snapper's head off with a butcher knife and pry the jaws apart with a screwdriver, and all the time it hurt like hell. Dillon kept teasing me to cry, but I wouldn't. That's when they started calling me Tuff.

Dillon. All my life I would be remembering him.

"He's dead," I said to Mom.

She stood there blinking at me. "Shawn." At least she knew who I was, though she called me by my real name for some reason. "What happened to your face? Did I do that?"

"Forget my face! Dillon got killed. Up the mountain. Somebody set a gun trap and killed him."

I saw her stiffen as she finally got it. She stood there a minute, very still. "Dillon's dead?" she said.

"Yes, goddammit!"

But then she shrugged and took another swig of beer. "Huh," she said. "Well, one less to worry about."

I swear to God that is just what she said.

Something snapped inside me like a bone breaking—except it was not a bone, it was my mind.

Then the parts fell into a kind of pattern, and I knew what I had to do.

I turned around and walked into the trailer and pulled a brown paper grocery bag out from behind the refrigerator to pack in. I didn't have much. None of us did. I wouldn't need more than one bag.

I headed for the little room I shared with Dillon—used to share with Dillon—and I saw his old Garth Brooks shirt he liked to sleep in hanging down from his rumpled-up bunk, and my heart turned over. It was like he was in there.

But he wasn't. He was dead, and somebody ought to notice. I yanked open my dresser drawer and threw my spare clothes into my bag.

Mom came in. "Where the hell you think you're going?"

"I am going to find whoever killed him." I slammed the drawer shut. "When I get the son of a bitch, I am going to kill him the same way."

There was junk on top of the dresser, maybe some of it mine. I pawed through it and came up with a snapshot of me and Dillon with that damn bike, and I held it in my hand and started shaking. He was so proud of that bike. Bought it himself with money he saved. Gave me a ride on it into town every day after school, so I wouldn't have to be around the trailer when the old man came home.

"Shawn, don't be an idiot," Mom said, acting kind of sober now. "Let bad enough alone. Dillon's better off."

I whispered, "You bitch." Didn't she give a shit about anybody?

"You expect me to be sorry about him? I ain't sorry. He got off easy." She was determined not to cry for him, ever, I could tell that. Goddammit, she ought to cry for him. Somebody had to, and I wasn't going to do it. I was sixteen years old, and I was going to kill somebody, not cry.

I told my mother, "You may go to hell."

"I'm already there," she said.

No damn joke. The noise of her five bawling brats came right up through all the holes rusted in the trailer she lived in with her stick-up-the-ass old man.

She asked, "Where you heading?"

"Out of here. Anywhere but here." I put Dillon's picture in my pocket, turned my back, and went.

"Hey!" she hollered after me from the trailer door. "You might want to look up a guy named Pen Leppo."

This was strange—she wasn't the drop-in-and-visit type. She wasn't the hinting type, either, but it sounded to me like she was hinting at something. Altogether it was odd enough so that I turned around to look back at her.

"Penrose Leppo," she said. "Tell him I said hi."

"Why?"

She yelled like she hated me, "He's your father."

2

I hiked back to Sid's Mountain and walked up to the place where Dillon had died. I set down my paper bag and stood around there awhile in the dusk. The shotgun was gone. Cops must have taken it with them. Dillon gone, murder weapon gone, everything gone except trees standing there and yellow police tape shutting me out.

Birds were bedding down in the trees, chirping like nothing had happened. I hated them. I hated everything.

I whispered like my brother was there. "Dillon, I'm going to get the son of a bitch."

It didn't help. I tried to think how to do it, how to find the killer, but it was no good. I couldn't think, couldn't swear, couldn't do anything. Couldn't even scream.

The birds screamed. *Crack*—a rifle fired not far away. And it was not hunting season.

The bullet whistled close by me and whanged off a tree beside the Jeep trail. I jumped and ran before my mind caught up to what was happening.

Somebody was gunning, and I was the game.

He fired once more, but by then I was behind a rock pile and plunging down the mountain. It was rough country, steep, thick, not a part of the mountain where I had ever been before. Good deer-hunting country, but I didn't much like being the deer.

There was a little cabin back there. The way it was set deep in a stand of hemlocks, I was almost on top of it before I saw it.

It wasn't a real good time to stop and visit, considering that somebody was trying to kill me. Didn't look like anybody was home anyway. Dark. I ran on past, then stopped running and walked. Why should I be scared? As if I really cared whether some guy shot me.

Probably the same guy who had murdered Dillon.

I walked faster, because it did matter whether I stayed alive. I had to find out who he was and kill him.

When I got to the road I kept heading upriver, away from home, and just walked.

Miles, hours, until I wore myself out and could think a little.

I thought just enough to stop at a phone booth in Quarryville and use the book to look up Pen Leppo.

Whaddaya know—he was in there. *Leppo Penrose G. 216 Main DmShm.* That meant Dam Shame. It was the name of the town, Dam Shame, because it sat right by a dam on the river and the dam was named Shame after some government guy.

Ten miles ahead.

I kept walking. Didn't know what else to do. I hurt too bad to get really original in my thinking. All I knew was, sooner or later I would need a place to sleep and something to eat, so I was heading to see this Leppo guy. Anyhow, I wanted . . . something. Dillon, mostly.

Dillon when he is about twelve years old and I am about ten, both of us jumping from boat to boat, down at the boat rental place, with the sun frying our backs while we're looking under the seats for dropped fishhooks or sinkers or bobbers or pennies or anything else we can use. Dillon keeping an eye out for the hairy-chin woman who might chase us off. Neither of us finding much.

"We don't have to keep doing this," I say, getting tired of it. "Our dad is gonna come and give us each a new fishing rod and a tackle box full of spinners and stuff. All we'll have to do is dig bait."

"He might as well give us money for bait while he's at it," Dillon says.

"Sure! He can give us each a thousand dollars, and we can buy our own fishing rods and our own boat."

Dillon is tired, too. "Where the hell would he get a thousand dollars?"

"He's, uh, he's a stunt man for the movies. Or, no, he's a movie star himself." I have this idea my father is tall and husky and blond, like Schwarzenegger or somebody, real macho, but he would be my friend if somebody reminded him about me.

"Dream on, Tuff." Dillon doesn't want to play the game. "Come on, this is no good." He leads me up to the snack stand, where at least there's some shade, and we get down to look for dropped money in the dirt and grass. My stomach is growling and the hot dogs smell like heaven, but we will never find enough money to buy one.

"We need a metal detector," Dillon says.

Sure. That's at least as impossible as my daydreams.

"Tuff?"

I'm not talking.

"Maybe he's a stunt man and a movie star," Dillon says. "Huh, Tuff?" He's going along with it now, to make me happy.

"Okay, and he flies a seaplane," I say. "He's going to come flying in and land right on the river and call out our names so we can grab a boat and go climb in the plane with him. In just a minute now."

"Right, Tuff," Dillon says. There is no plane and no metal detector, either. The river is slipping by just like it's been doing for ten thousand years, and we are on our knees in the grass, and we look at each other's sunburned faces and laugh like loons.

It was strange, that night I walked to Dam Shame. I sure as hell didn't have time for stupid daydreams anymore—I mean, face it, why

19

should I have that kind of father? I'm not tall or good looking, and I'm not much of a fighter or much good at sports or hunting or school or anything. I'm nothing special in any way. I knew the score. And Dillon—nothing could make up for losing Dillon. But behind all that, the old dreams were still there, stronger than ever. It was like, since something so bad had happened, now I was expecting a personal miracle just to balance things out.

There had already been a miracle. After all the years of not knowing, I finally knew. I knew who my father was.

Somehow he had to make it all better.

It was real late when I got there. After midnight. Cars with drunks yipping and hollering in them roared past sometimes, but there were no lights in the houses, no people on the street.

I found number 216, and it was one of those half-assed shacks that call themselves stores and sell a little of everything, including bait. Especially bait—fishing is good below Shame Dam. MEAL WORMS said some signs on the front. NIGHT CRAWLERS. SANDWICHES 79¢. MINNOWS, SHINERS, LEECHES.

I looked at the house number about five times. The streetlight showed it fine. This was it.

So much for personal miracles.

I thought about turning away again—it might be better not knowing. But the tug was too strong. This stupid father thing, it had been like an undercurrent in my whole life, so strong I couldn't seem to go against it. I had to do it. I knocked on the door.

I waited. Nobody came.

I knocked again, pretty loud. According to the phone book, the guy lived here. If he was asleep in the back, I had to knock loud to wake him up.

Nobody answered.

It would have made sense to go away, sleep in a boat or something, come back the next day. But why should anything make sense when Dillon was dead? My brother was gone, I finally knew who my father was, and my dream idea of him was going down the drain. I went a little crazy, I was so tired and sad and mad. "Goddammit, let me in!" I yelled, and I started pounding on the door, whamming it with my fists, kicking it.

Nothing happened. Nobody came. Not even a light came on.

"Goddammit all to hell!" I aimed a punch at the display window and put my fist through it. Glass fell down with a sound like little bells.

I kicked some more glass away until there was a hole big enough to get through if I bent over, and that's what I did. I went in. I was so gonzo, I had broken in.

The inside of the store was dark and all cluttered up with shelves full of junk. I stood there panting and shaking a little as I calmed down and started to get scared.

Dammit, I was an idiot. I needed to get out of there.

"Don't move," said a man's voice.

A light went on, and there he was.

He was a short, chubby guy, bald, in a pair of baggy striped boxer shorts, with a pistol in his hand, pointed at me. I was so bummed I just looked at him a minute, not even afraid of the gun.

"Pen Leppo?" I asked.

He kind of nodded, staring back. God, he looked like the Gerber baby, standing there all pudgy and pale. But what the hell did I expect? A guy named Penrose, for God's sake. Living in a place like Dam Shame.

"I'm Shawn Lacey," I told him, flat out. "My mom is Candy Lacey. She says you're my father."

He kept staring. I guess maybe at the broken

window and the blood dripping down from my hand. Maybe at my long hair—there was never money for a barber, but mostly I grew it to annoy my mom's old man. Maybe at my patched-up face. Later on he told me he didn't really take it in all at once, he was trying to decide whether to call the cops—some long-haired punk kid had broken into his place— or offer me a hankie, because I looked like I needed one.

I just stared back. Hell, I had all night. It wasn't like I was going anywhere.

He looked maybe forty years old, a little older than my mom. Not much chin. Not much chest hair. I wouldn't have thought she would go for him—he wasn't her type. Of course, they hadn't stayed together.

"What's your name again?" he asked finally. He still had the gun pointed at me.

"Shawn Lacey."

"You're Candy Lacey's kid?"

I nodded. The reason my last name was the same as hers was not because she had ever married anybody. It was because she had *not* ever married anybody. I figured he knew that. Most people seemed to know it.

But he knew more than I thought. "You had

a brother Dillon?" he asked, real gentle and quiet. "Got killed today?" He must have heard it on the news.

I had to close my eyes for a minute, and I guess my face changed. When I looked again he was lowering the gun. He put it in a drawer, locked it, and walked over to me.

"How's your mom?" he asked.

"Fine." She was probably dead drunk, but I didn't have to tell that to this Pen Leppo guy.

"She says I'm your father?"

I nodded, looking down at his bare feet. His toes were fat. Feet are stupid-looking things. So was his bare soft belly, stupid looking. My throat felt tight, like I couldn't talk, yet I didn't want him to hug me or anything. I didn't want anybody to touch me.

He didn't. His hands stayed down by his sides. "Well," he said softly, "she must have some reason for saying that."

I looked from his belly to his face, which didn't show me much. It was serious, that was all. But at least he wasn't screaming and calling the cops and kicking my ass the way he had a right to.

"You can clean up this mess in the morning," he told me, watching where he stepped because of the broken glass. "Come on in here for now."

He took me to a little kitchen in the back. He made me stand at the sink while he ran cold water over my hand to make sure all the glass was out of the cuts. Then he ran a basin full of warm water and dish-soap suds, and he made me stick my hand in there and soak it a couple minutes so it wouldn't get infected. After all that he wrapped it up in some sort of damn Boy Scout white bandage and motioned me to sit down at the table. "You eat lately?" he asked.

It was a simple question, but I couldn't think of the answer.

Pen Leppo went ahead and put some chicken noodle soup in a bowl and nuked it in his microwave. When it was hot he set it in front of me, and I guess I looked at it like I didn't know what it was. Not that there was anything wrong with it. His kitchen was cleaner than Mom's. I just couldn't think what food was good for.

"Eat it," he said.

I picked up the spoon he gave me and ate one mouthful. Then I puked it right back up. I sat there puking and puking into the bowl, even though there was nothing in me to throw up. After I finally quit puking I felt so bad I put my head down on the table and just stayed that way. I didn't want to move ever again.

"Shawn," Pen said.

He wasn't much to look at, but his voice was powerful. Quiet, but it made me drag myself up. The mess was gone. Pen was sitting across the table from me, still bare chested, leaning back in his chair.

"Tell me," he said.

I looked at him.

"Just tell me about it from the start. Tell me everything that happened."

It was real late. The night was still and so was he. Something about him made me able to do it. Maybe it was the way he didn't say too much. Maybe it was the way that soft bare chest of his seemed to soak it all in. I told him the whole thing—about Dillon taking me to town on his dirt bike and teasing me about liking this girl, about the way he died. About Mom being drunk and not caring. About leaving, and going back up the mountain, and somebody shooting at me. Probably the same guy who killed Dillon.

"I am going to find out who it was and do

him the way he did my brother," I said. "I am going to find him and kill him."

"No, you are not," Pen Leppo said, which was the first time he had tried to tell me what to do. "A lot of good it'll do Dillon if you go to jail."

"I don't give a shit! Even if the cops get the guy he'll only get manslaughter, which is what, two years? Five years? Dillon's dead, and this guy gets his butt smacked? I am going to kill him."

"You better just worry about your own butt first," Pen said quietly. "You better call the cops first thing in the morning and tell them where you are. They'll be looking at you funny if they think you ran away."

It sounded like I was staying with him at least for a while, so maybe I better do some of what he said. I mumbled, "Okay."

"You think you can go to sleep now? Let's find you a place to sleep."

Behind the store he had two rooms, with his bed in one and his kitchen and TV and a sofa in the other. He put me on the sofa, and he kept bringing me pillows and covers and things, like he wanted to tuck me in. I kind of wished he would just go away and let me alone, and I kind of wished he would stay and hold my hand or something. No, not my hand. It hurt from smashing my way in.

"I'm sorry about your window," I said. It was hard to talk. I felt really tired.

"Forget it. We'll fix it."

"I'm not usually like that."

"You had kind of a bad day," he said, real dry. "Forget it. Go to sleep. If you need anything, come get me."

I had lost my bag of stuff up on the mountain, but I still had my picture of Dillon in my pants pocket, thank God. If there was a God. I didn't feel like there was.

After Pen Leppo was gone I got the picture out and looked at it in the dark. I couldn't see Dillon's face.

3

The church bells made me mad, waking me up the next morning. Dillon was dead and the God pushers wouldn't even let me sleep. Let somebody drive through with their stereo too loud and it's terrible, but the churches can bing-bong the whole town whenever they want to. It pissed me off.

Pen Leppo heard me swearing and came and stood over me. He was dressed already. "I take it you're not going to church," he said.

"*No.*"

"Okay, but get up and call the cops."

"You call them."

"Better if you do it yourself."

He kept after me and made me do it, and then he made me take a shower. "Just don't get your face wet. That splint on your nose will come off." He found me a package of underwear in that junked-up store of his. Then, after I was clean, he changed my bandages and made me eat. Toast. Cereal with milk. I wasn't hungry, but I forced the stuff down and it stayed down.

"We ought to go see your mother," Pen said, sitting there and watching me eat.

Some things he couldn't make me do. I set my spoon down. "No way."

"Shawn, she'll be sober now, she'll be hurting. I tried to call her and tell her where you were, but—"

"She don't have no phone." What did he think we were, rich like him? He had a car, a beat-up '65 Dodge—I saw it parked outside under a propped-up piece of rusty roof, next to a row of stinky old bathtubs I guessed he raised his worms in. He had his store, TV, microwave, shower, a coin laundry right down the street to wash his clothes at. I mean, along the river that's a lot. People living on the river don't generally have much. Some of us even less than others. Like my mother. I wondered whether having nothing had made her a slut, or if being a slut had made her have nothing. Like most of the things I wondered about, it didn't matter.

"She don't give a shit about me anyway," I told Pen.

"I have reason to think she does. Anyway, I

give a shit about her. We have to let her know you're okay."

"You go see her if you want to," I told him. "I don't ever want to see her again." I meant it.

"You'll have to, at the funeral."

"What funeral?" My voice went up so high it broke. "How the hell would we have a funeral? We got no money." Funerals were for people with enough to pay the undertaker. "The cops get done with Dillon, they're going to throw him in the garbage!" The thought made me so sick I screamed it.

"Huh," Pen said, and his face got real thoughtful.

"I keep yelling at you," I said. "I don't mean to yell at you." I didn't want to be that way to my father. I might not want to hug him or anything, but I didn't have to yell at him. "Excuse me." I stood up and got out of there to calm down.

I went and swept up the broken glass in the store, and he let me alone. I found a piece of cardboard that was big enough and taped it over the broken place. While I was working, I thought how I was going to find out who killed Dillon. Being mad all the time was no use. Feeling bad was no use. I had to do something, ask around, ask questions. Go to bars, gun shops, bowling alleys, places where men hang out. Go back up the mountain and ask the people in that cabin if they saw anything. Get moving.

Pen was on the phone with somebody. When he got done and sat at the table again to drink some more coffee, I went in.

"Would you take me back to Sid's Mountain?" I asked, keeping it quiet and polite.

He looked up at me, still thoughtful. I noticed he looked better in the daylight, with clothes on. He wasn't a bad-looking father for a guy his age, just a little short, a little bald, a little flabby.

"I need to talk to some people," I said.

"Is your mother one of them?"

I shook my head.

"Forget it then, son." He didn't say it hard, but he meant it. He kept looking straight at me. "I know what you're thinking of doing. No way am I going to let you go nosing around and maybe get yourself killed. That's what we pay cops for."

"They already told me they don't know nothing!"

"That's what they have to say."

I wasn't going to start yelling at him again. I picked up the phone instead and called the cop I had talked to before, Detective Mohatt. "Anything yet on who killed Dillon?" I asked him.

"Shawn, I just told you a couple hours ago, these things take time." He sounded grouchy because I had phoned him again. Not the real patient sort.

"I forgot to ask you something," I said. "Dillon's bike, are you done with it? Can I have it back?"

"It's evidence, son," he said. "We're holding it awhile. Nice talking with you." Before he cut me off I heard him say to somebody in his office, "Christ, his brother's dead and all he can think about is getting his hands on the goddamn bike."

I hung up the phone, shaking mad. I needed the bike to get around on, to find the murderer, not for fun and games. That cop was a prick. For a couple minutes I just stood there breathing hard. Then I turned back to Pen Leppo.

"Look," I told him, "I have to do it. If you won't help me, I'm going to have to do it without you. I'm going to have to run off and sleep in a junked car or something, and I don't want that. I just found you, for God's sake."

33

I guess he could tell I meant it. "I don't want that, either," he said.

We stared at each other.

"Please," I said. My voice quivered. I didn't mean to get that way with him. It just happened.

"Okay, Shawn, you win. But listen." He stood up. He wasn't so short, actually—about as tall as me. "You don't do nothing by yourself. Only if I'm with you every step of the way."

We went to see my mother first. "You can sit in the car if that's what you gotta do," Pen said, and that's what I did. I made him park up along the road so the brats wouldn't come near me.

When Pen came out he had his lips pressed together. "It's bad in there," he said.

"I know."

"Your mom's in bad shape."

I knew what he wanted me to do, and no way could I do it. I couldn't look at her without wanting to kill her. "Start the damn car and get me out of here," I said.

He didn't do it, but he didn't say any more about Mom, either. He asked, "That boyfriend of hers ever hit you?"

"Once in a while." Not bad, not to put me in the hospital or anything. "Mostly he just takes it out on Dillon and me other ways."

" 'Takes it out'?"

"He don't like us being around." I couldn't seem to stop talking like Dillon was still alive. "Because we're not his. He's okay with his own kids." The little brats.

Pen got that thoughtful look of his. He scowled when he was thinking, but not like he was mad.

"No, it wasn't him," I said. I knew what Pen was thinking, wondering about Mom's old man. "He doesn't have the guts." At least I didn't think so. The guy drank a lot, and he got mean when he drank, but not that mean. Anyway, I couldn't see him rigging up that shotgun. Too much like work.

Pen started the car hard and blew us out of there. "Okay, where to?" he asked me.

We went from trailer to trailer, shack to shack. I'm not usually the kind to go up to strange people's houses and knock on their doors, but then Dillon was not usually dead, either. Whenever I found somebody home, I asked them if they'd seen anything or heard anything to tell who killed him. Nobody knew anything, but I got the feeling they would tell me what I needed to know if they could. These were river people. I know river people. Nobody outside cares about us much, including cops, and sometimes we don't even care about ourselves until something bad happens, but at least then we stick together. I didn't have to explain to anybody what had happened to Dillon. Everybody I talked with had already heard.

"Try a bar?" Pen suggested when we started running out of trailers and shacks.

"Closed on Sunday."

He rolled his eyes at himself. "Duh! Stupid." He started to shoot himself in the head with his finger, then got a peculiar look on his face and scratched his ear instead.

I knew what we had to do next. It had been hanging like a skeleton at the back of my mind all afternoon. I said, kind of low, "While it's still good and light I want to go up the mountain again. I want to show you where it happened and find out who lives in that cabin."

He got real serious right away. "Shawn, no."

"Maybe you can see something I didn't."

"Not goddamn likely. That's not what's going to happen, and you know it."

"So what's going to happen?" I asked him. "I don't know what's going to happen. That's what I've got to find out."

"You're crazy, you know that?"

I told him, "Look, you don't have to come," and I turned around and started hiking. We were parked not far from the foot of the Jeep trail. In a minute I heard him puffing along behind me, and I slowed down to let him catch up. He was out of shape.

Between puffs he said, "Don't—you care— if you get—yourself killed?"

I shook my head. It was the truth, I didn't. I wished it was me that had got killed in the first place. I wished it was me instead of Dillon.

"You care—if you get—me killed?"

I didn't answer, but I took us off the Jeep trail into the woods, where we had more cover, and I said, "Quiet." We eased along. I was always quiet in the woods, not rustling leaves, not breaking sticks, because I liked to see the animals. Kind of a habit. Pen knew how to walk that way, too. Probably he had been a hunter, maybe a good one—though I was no good, I always got buck fever. I saw deer but never shot them.

We didn't see or hear anything unusual. Crows yelled at us. I hate crows. They're like people who mind everybody else's business. The crows just had to tell everything and any-body on Sid's Mountain that we were coming.

I took us to the cabin first, because cutting through the woods it was kind of on the way. When I say *cabin* I don't mean a log cabin, but it wasn't a summer cottage, either, or a shack like some of the ones along the river. It was a tight little wood-shingled place, and there was a thread of smoke coming out of the stone chimney. Walking up, I thought I saw movement in a window. But when I knocked at the door nobody came.

I knocked again. "Open up, damn you," I muttered.

"Don't get yourself in a hissy fit," Pen said. I guess he was afraid I would try to put my fist through the door, like I did with his store window.

It was a strange place. I had lots of time to look around, waiting on the doorstep, and I noticed one thing especially: There was no driveway. Not even a dirt road leading in or out. Whoever lived here, didn't they ever go for groceries or anything?

"Come on," Pen said. "Nobody's home."

"He's in there," I said. "I can smell him." I was almost sure I had heard somebody moving around inside. But there was nothing we could do about it, so we left.

"Watch for snakes," I told Pen as we headed

up the mountain. I didn't want him putting his hand in a nest of copperheads as we climbed the rocks.

Pen was puffing hard by the time we got up the steep rocky part, so I stopped to let him breathe. I could see yellow streaks of police tape through the trees. We were close. I looked around and listened, but I couldn't hear anything except Pen panting.

Still hidden in the woods, we walked close enough for him to see. "Here it is," I whispered.

He nodded and stood looking at—nothing, really. A square of mountainside. A dirt track with maybe a little blood fertilizing it. What the hell was I expecting him to tell me?

"The son of a bitch rigged a shotgun up there," I whispered, pointing, trying to explain. "About four and a half feet above the ground. With string across the road for somebody to break. Black, so they wouldn't see it till it was too late."

Pen nodded some more, and we moved around a little. Then we saw something else.

"Jeez," I said, "there's my clothes." Downhill a few yards, outside the taped-off area, a brown paper bag was still sitting on the Jeep track.

"That's yours?" Pen whispered.

"Uh-huh."

"I'm surprised the cops didn't take it."

"Like I told you, they don't give a shit. They haven't even been up here."

"But I thought you told them you got shot at."

"I did." We weren't whispering anymore. We had both forgotten to be afraid. I walked out of the woods, grabbed my bag of clothes, and picked it up the way I'd carry a sack of groceries, between my arm and my chest.

"Don't move!" Pen shouted.

I froze, because I felt it at the same time he saw it: something squirming around in the bag.

"Don't move, Tuff," Pen said quietly. How did he know to call me that? From my mother, probably. "Don't blink, don't breathe. It's a big granddaddy copperhead, and he's poking his head out right by your face. Don't move."

I tried to do what he said. I clenched my teeth and tried to hold still, even though I wanted to shake and scream. I'm not any more afraid of snakes than the average person, but this was different. I could feel the snake's muscles bulging through the paper bag. I could feel his forked tongue sniffing my neck.

"Just hang on," Pen said. "Hold real still." I

could hear by his voice that he was inching close.

I stared straight ahead, not moving my eyes to look even when Pen eased close enough that I could see him, because I was afraid I might move my head. God, I was afraid.

Pen soft-footed up until he was only a couple feet away, almost close enough for the snake to get him, too. "Okay," he said, "when I say, you drop the bag and jump. Okay?" The way he asked a question, I almost nodded, but just in time he warned, "Don't move!" and I caught myself. "Not until I say," he told me. "I'm waiting for him to come out a little farther. . . ."

I was so scared I felt sick.

Then out of the corner of my eye I saw a flash, a blur.

"Now! Jump!"

I jumped like a rabbit. I think I threw the bag more than dropped it. But even before I did anything, Pen had the copperhead. I wouldn't have believed he could move that fast. The blur I had seen was his hand. He had grabbed the snake right behind its head, and he stood there holding it. It didn't seem to bother him the way the thing was hissing and thrashing around, even though it was almost as long as he was tall.

"Don't go near that bag yet," he told me, and he walked into the woods with the snake, then came back without it.

"You okay, son?"

I nodded. "Thanks," I whispered. I could barely talk. My heart was pounding, and I felt shaky. I guess I wanted to live after all.

"You're welcome." Pen found himself a stick and started poking at the bag to see if something else would come out.

Off in the woods, not too far away, somebody laughed. It was not a real laugh but the put-on kind, a bad-guy laugh meant for us to hear.

Pen looked at me, and I looked at him, and we got out of there. The heck with my clothes. We didn't stop running until we were halfway to the river road.

Then we walked awhile and caught our breath. When we were almost to the road, I said what I was thinking. "Copperheads don't just crawl into paper bags for fun."

"They might," Pen said, "but I don't think that one did."

I nodded. If it wasn't for hearing that laugh, I might have thought finding a snake having a nap in my spare shirts was an accident. But the laugh had made it pretty clear: no accident. That copperhead was a message for me.

4

What the hell were you doing up there?" Detective Mohatt yelled at me over the phone when I told him about the copperhead and the guy laughing. "Just stay away from there."

That night he and a couple other cops came and asked me questions. Did I have enemies? Did Dillon have enemies? Tell them again how Dillon got killed. Was Dillon having a fight with anybody? Was he having a fight with me?

"No," I whispered. These guys were sick. Sure, Dillon and I fought sometimes, but— what they were thinking was sick.

"Over a girl, maybe?"

"No, dammit! I don't have a girl."

"But he did."

Sure, because he was special. He wore T-shirts cut up to show his muscles, a chrome chain for a belt, black jeans, wild black hair, a million-dollar smile. "He had plenty. So what? He was my brother. Don't you guys get it?" My voice rose.

"Shawn," Pen said quietly, to shush me, and I shut up, but only because he wanted me to. I owed him.

Mohatt said, "They call you Tuff, right?"

"Yes." It came out real hard.

"Just don't get too damn tough with us, son."

The cops went away finally, but I couldn't get to sleep. When Pen was asleep I got up and went outside, closing the door softly so I wouldn't wake him, and walked across the street and through somebody's yard to the riverbank. The spillway noise was loud in my ears, and I didn't like the way the dam locked up the river into just another boring lake. I walked down to below the dam, and that was better, more like the river I was used to. The water was about a mile wide, but shallow, full of wild islands and white rapids and quartz rocks and light. I stood there a long time, just looking. In the rock pools below the dam the bass would be swarming, drunk with water rush and air bubbles. If Dillon was there we'd go wading out in the moonlight and try to catch them with our bare hands.

How could he be gone? He was everywhere. In the night. In the light on the river. In every breath I took.

Yet he was nowhere. Breathing hurt. Living hurt.

Nobody understood. The cops didn't understand. Damn them, they weren't going to find Dillon's killer. I had to do it. I wouldn't be able to sleep until I did.

I did go back to bed and doze some, on toward morning.

Monday. I hate Mondays. Pen woke me up and said, "Don't you have school?"

I shook my head.

"C'mon, Shawn, it's April, for God's sake. I know you have school."

"I'm not going." Maybe I would just quit. Go drinking on weekends and bash mailboxes. Get a job at a car wash, like Dillon. No, have a nighttime career, like stealing stereos out of cars. Get arrested. Spend the rest of my life in jail.

"Okay, but get up."

Damn, he could be a pain in the ass. Of course, the guy was my father, so what did I expect. I got up.

"Can we go nose around some more?" I asked him over breakfast.

"You think you can stay away from poisonous reptiles and gunfire?"

"I'll stay away from Sid's Mountain." For now. Before I went back I needed to find out who lived in that cabin. And I needed to have a plan.

And a weapon, probably.

Pen said, "I've got a store to run, son. After closing time we can go someplace."

I moped around until he put me to work. He showed me how to feed the worms with coffee grounds and other kinds of garbage he collected from the neighbors. Feeding worms was not a high point in my life, especially since the way they writhed around reminded me of the copperhead, but Pen seemed to almost like them. After we were done with the worms, he sent me to dig weeds out of the cracks in the sidewalk while he made a bunch of phone calls. Then he gave me some money out of his cash drawer and sent me down the street to the Goodwill store to get myself a change of clothes. I had been in the same shirt and pants for three days. The Goodwill store isn't exactly the fashion place to shop, but where I come from we don't take no trips to Paris, so who cares. I found a couple things that kind of fit and came back with them and put them on.

We had hot dogs for lunch. They reminded me of the worms. I didn't eat much. After Pen ate he said, "Listen, Shawn, do you think you can run the store for a couple hours? I gotta go get some glass to replace the window."

I said, "I should have gone to school."

He grinned so wide I had to smile. I said, "Okay, go get your glass already."

He was gone more than a couple hours. People came in for milk and bait and stuff, but I still had plenty of time to be bored. That place was not exactly hopping with business. The store was empty in late afternoon when a girl who looked familiar walked in.

My chest started to ache when I saw her, but I couldn't think why. I couldn't think who she was.

She came straight up to me and said, "Tuff, how you doing?" The way she said it, like she meant it, told me she knew about Dillon.

"Okay. I'm doing all right, I guess." Who *was* she?

She saw it in my face and said, "You don't remember me, do you? Monica. Monica Zarfos. I know you from school."

Okay, that kind of explained it. She was one of those girls you see in the halls without really noticing. Plain brownish hair pulled back. Plain face. Short legs. Baggy clothes. Probably had all the right body parts, but I'd never know from looking at her in those clothes. Nothing special about her.

Yeah, knowing her from school kind of explained it, but not really. Why did seeing her make me hurt all over?

Monica said, "You came to my place to phone the ambulance."

Oh, my God.

She said, "I went back up the mountain with you. I know you don't remember. You were in shock."

Damn straight.

She said, "After I saw what happened to Dillon, I went home and cried. I cried till I was sick."

My heart went hot. Hearing her say it made me want to cry myself, and hug her and kiss her and laugh all at once, because somebody cared besides me.

I didn't do any of those things, but I blurted out, "You want something to eat?"

We got Scooter Crunch bars out of the store's freezer and sat on the steps out front to eat them. I figured Pen wouldn't mind. Too bad if he did. But I figured he wouldn't.

Monica asked me, "So how are you, really?"

"You came here to see me? Not to buy worms or something?"

"Noooo, I came to buy worms. Jeez." She wasn't mad, just teasing. "Would you answer my question? Are you going to be okay?"

"I guess." I hadn't thought about me much. "I just want to find out who killed him."

"I heard." She pulled her lips back from her teeth to bite off bits of her ice cream. "I heard you were asking around. That's what everybody wants, to get the guy who did him. You should have heard people talking in school today. Nobody's talking about anything else."

I should have gone to school, no damn joke. I asked, "What were they saying?"

"Lots of stuff." Monica started to smile, but not like she was happy. "You should have seen it. There's about six girls all crying and saying they were his girlfriend and fighting with each other over who gets to wear black."

I have to admit I was interested. "Who?"

She told me some names. "Did he really go with any of them?"

"No." Maybe he played around with them, but he would have told me if he really liked somebody.

"That makes me feel a little better. I—I had kind of a crush on Dillon." She was looking down, not at me. She sat there with her ice cream melting over her hands, and I didn't

49

know what to say. She missed him, too. In a weird way that made me feel better and very grateful to her. But I didn't know how to tell her what I felt.

So I got a napkin and wiped one of her hands. She looked at me and took the napkin and finished the job herself.

"It's no big deal," she said.

I tried to make conversation. "So what else is going on in school?"

"Oh, the Student Council took up a collection for the funeral, and the guidance counselor made one of those If-you-need-to-talk-I'm-here announcements, you know—"

"Wait a minute." Had I heard her right? "They're collecting money for a funeral for Dillon?"

"Sure. A lot of people are. There's cans and boxes in all the stores. Didn't you know about it?" Monica sat blinking at me.

"No. No, I didn't."

"Well, there are."

"Jeez," I said, "people are gonna give him a real funeral?"

"Looks like it." Then she eyed my Goodwill pants.

"You thinking maybe I better get some real clothes to wear?"

"Well, yeah," she said, "maybe you better," and the look she gave me was so funny that all of a sudden I was laughing. We were both laughing. I wouldn't have believed I could laugh like that anymore.

A rusty old Chevy came down the street. "There's my ride," Monica said, and she jumped up.

"Wait, Monica." I stood up and stretched out my hand to her. "Come back. I've got to ask you something. Who do they think killed Dillon?"

She turned to look at me. Her ride was stopped in the middle of the road, waiting.

"Monica," I begged.

She stared at me like she was scared, and then she was gone.

Pen came back with a pane of glass packaged in cardboard so big it stuck out of his trunk. "How much did that cost you?" I wanted to know. For some reason his insurance didn't cover it. I had asked.

"Never damn mind."

I said, "More than this store makes in a week, right? Tell me how much. I want to pay you back."

"Just never goddamn mind, Shawn." He was

busy trying to get the glass out of his car without breaking it.

I took a couple steps closer and I said, "Listen, somebody told me people are taking up a collection for a funeral for Dillon."

"That right?" He stopped messing with the glass a minute and looked owl eyed at me. "We'll have to get a jar or something in here."

He didn't fool me. Sometimes he could see right through me, and sometimes I could see right through him. "You turkey," I said to him, "you put it together, didn't you? All those phone calls."

He didn't say yes or no, just got real embarrassed, like I'd caught him with his pants down.

I said, "Thanks." Damn my throat closing up on me again. I couldn't say any more.

He was barn red. "Damn it, Tuff, you don't need to thank me. Just help me with this goddamn glass." I got hold of the other end of it, and we wrestled the thing out of the car and carried it around front. A couple minutes later he said, "If I had my druthers I would have just done it myself." The funeral, he meant. "But I don't have any money, either."

"Is it—do you think there's going to be enough?"

"Looks like. Anyway, the undertaker says no rush to pay him."

So there really was going to be a funeral. "When . . . ?"

"Thursday. The coroner released the body to your mom today."

"Where?"

"At the funeral parlor."

"I mean, where they going to bury him?"

"Oh. I got the Gardens to contribute a plot."

He said it like it was nothing, and it was the nicest cemetery I knew of, on a hill by the river, one of those places that don't have head-stones, just little markers, so it looks like a park. A real classy place. Thinking about it put me in kind of a daze while I helped Pen pull the old glass out of the window and fit the new glass in and putty it in place, him on one side and me on the other. We couldn't talk to each other. He smiled at me now and then.

We had chicken sandwiches for supper, and for once I was hungry. After we were done eating I asked him, "Why?"

"Why what?"

"Why did you do it for Dillon?"

He gave me a funny look.

"I mean, I guess if you're my dad, then

you're Dillon's dad, too." This was hard to talk about. "Were, I mean. But . . ."

I wanted to ask him a lot of things. How long had he and Mom been together? Why had they split up? Where had he been since? Why hadn't he come to see us? Why hadn't he been a father to us? He seemed like the kind of guy who would have at least tried. And now he was taking care of his kid's funeral when he hadn't taken care of the kid. It was strange.

But I didn't feel like I could ask him any of those questions. I liked him a lot, but I hadn't ever called him *Dad*. In some ways I felt really close to him, but in other ways it was like there was a glass wall between us.

He sat back drinking his coffee and watching me, and he said, "Tuff. Tell me about Dillon."

"Huh?"

"Just tell me about him."

"I—I dunno what you mean. What about him?"

"Anything. What was he like?"

I got out my photo of Dillon and me and showed it to him. "No wonder he had girls," Pen said. "Good looking."

"Yeah."

"You're going to look just like him in a couple of years."

"Sure. Tell me another."

"You are. I mean it. So what was he like? Was he fun to have around?"

"God, yes." All of a sudden I understood what he meant, what was Dillon like. "He would do crazy things. We used to sneak out at night and hitch a ride to Quarryville, or go dock fishing, or sneak a rowboat from the rental place and go to the islands. By moonlight." I started to grin, remembering. "We used to make fires and chase each other through the trees. We found an island with Indian rock carvings on it once, but we could never find it again. We used to let the current take us clear down to Confluence sometimes. Then we had to row upstream, and we wouldn't get back until morning, and the boat rental people would threaten to call the cops, and Mom would scream at us."

Pen sat there smiling. "So you were a pair of river rats," he said.

"We sure were. We used to go swim in the river at night. Under all them stars. . . ." I couldn't think how to make him see the way it had been, but maybe he knew how the water felt warm and every sound echoed beautiful and the fish flashed silver in the water. "Swam up to some guys poaching deer onshore once,

and they thought we were beaver or something—they shone the light in our eyes and
we scared them. They ran like they'd seen
ghosts."

Pen sat there for hours, listening while I told
him about Dillon. I told him about the worst
thing Dillon ever did to me, which was when
I was little and he gave me one of those choc-
olate laxatives and told me it was candy. I told
him about one of the best things Dillon ever
did for me, which was not too long ago, helping
me out when Mom's old man came after me
with a belt. If the drunk son of a bitch had
tried to whip me, I would have fought him,
and God knows what would have happened.
I'm not little, but I'm sure not big enough to
take that ape. But Dillon stepped in, and the
yutz knew he couldn't fight both of us.

"Dillon stood up to that gorilla?" Pen said,
impressed. "That's something. I wouldn't
want to do it."

"You'd rather grab a copperhead with your
bare hands, huh?" The man had saved my life.
Even Dillon had never done that.

"That was nothing. That was easy. Handling
a mean drunk is hard."

We talked till Pen yawned and said, "Time
for bed."

I jumped up. "You told me we were going to go ask around at bars and stuff tonight!"

"It's kind of late for that now, son."

For a minute I just about hated him. "That's what you wanted, isn't it? To keep me here, keep me talking, make me forget what I gotta do?"

He was watching me in that quiet way of his. He said, "Tuff, c'mon. Give me a little credit. Chill out."

"Damn you," I said, and I went to the sofa and lay there spitting mad while he sighed and told me good night and went to bed. I didn't sleep much, just lay there in a rage at him and myself. I damn near decided to lift his keys and borrow his car and go cruise the bars on my own, the way Dillon and I used to borrow boats. I didn't have a license, but I knew how to drive. Had been borrowing cars and driving back roads since I was thirteen. Trouble was, probably they wouldn't have let me into the bars. Pen would have had to be with me.

Dammit. I was going to have to wait another day. Only one thing helped me calm down a little, which was that I promised myself I would get some answers at school in the morning.

5

Tuff, how are you doing, dude? You making it okay?"

"Tuff, everybody's really sorry. We all want you to know we're sorry."

"Tuff, you okay, man?"

My chest ached, my eyes stung, and I didn't want to be that way. I didn't want kids seeing me soft. I needed to be hard, like a snapping turtle armored in its shell. I needed to remember what I had to do for Dillon.

"Tuff, is there anything we can do?"

Just tell me who killed him.

I didn't say it, but I thought it, and it helped. Without the anger to hold me together I felt watery, like I wasn't solid; it was so strange being there with the school looking just the same when everything had changed.

"Tuff, we're so sorry about what happened."

"Tuff, if we can do anything. . . ."

"Thanks," I said to kids, moving toward my

locker. "I'm okay. Thanks. No, not really. Sure, I'll call you if I think of anything."

Just tell me who killed him!

I kept looking for Monica, and finally I saw her, hanging back, blending in with the crowd. I wanted to go over to her, but kids kept coming up to me, getting in my face. There were a couple of girls hanging on to me, crying, telling me they had loved Dillon.

JUST TELL ME WHO KILLED HIM!

"Do you think it was the mountain man?" some twitchy kid asked me.

My heart pounded so hard I could hear it in my ears. I wanted to grab the kid by the throat. I managed not to do that, and I didn't scream—because I almost lost my voice. I croaked at him, "Who?"

"You know, the mountain man. He lives up there in a cave or something." The twitchy kid grinned. He had scummy yellow teeth. "Eats raw meat. Hardly ever comes down."

"He does not eat raw meat," said a girl. "Why would he eat raw meat?"

"Hey, he's crazy," somebody else said. A bunch of them had followed me into homeroom and were clustered around. What a way to get popular. "I saw him in town once. All he is, is skin and bones and dirty clothes and a big old beard with spooky eyes looking out of it, you know?"

I had heard about him before, I'd just forgotten. River people don't pay that much attention to hillbilly stories. But you'd better believe I was paying attention now.

"He doesn't live in a cave," some guy said. "It's just a cabin."

"Yeah, but it's way back there. No road leading up to it. He only comes out twice a year. Anybody comes near it, he chases them away."

"On Sid's Mountain?" I asked.

"Yep."

I knew where he lived. I knew that cabin.

"He chased my dad with a gun once," some kid said. "My dad was deer hunting and got too close to his cabin, and he ran him off."

It had to be, it had to be, it had to be. I'd known all along that the cops were wrong, thinking it had something to do with Dillon and me, enemies and all that crap. That wasn't it at all. Anybody could have run into that gun trap. No, it was something about the place, the mountain, not about us kids—that was why I kept going back there. Somebody had put that shotgun in that tree. Somebody wanted to keep that mountaintop to themselves. And it made sense that it would be a crazy mountain man.

"My dad says he's an escaped prisoner, that's why he hides up there," some girl said. "He's wanted for murder in Mexico or somewhere. One of those countries where they still shoot people."

That was what I was going to do to him: shoot him. Blast him with a shotgun. Watch him bleed. Kill him the way he killed my brother.

No. Slower. A lot slower.

I don't know how I made it through the day. Every minute, my blood was rushing like a dam had just burst somewhere. I wanted like fire to go kill the guy—I wanted to do it right away—but I knew I had to wait. Be smart. Take time to think about it. Do it right. Do something right for once in my life.

During lunch period, I spotted Monica sitting on the edge of a group, and I shook loose of the crowd around me and went over to talk to her. I felt like coffee in one of those insulated cups, boiling hot on the inside, trying to stay cool on the outside. I had to talk to somebody, and for some reason I felt like I could trust

Monica. "Kids think they know who set the trap," I told her kind of fierce. "They're saying it was some mountain man."

She looked up at me with wide, scared eyes. "Shawn, don't listen to them. Don't believe them."

That hit me in the gut for a minute. It had to be serious when she called me by my real name. I sat down across from her. Maybe she knew something I didn't. "Do you know him?"

"No." She shook her head. "No, I don't know a thing about him. What I mean is, neither does anybody else. It's all just talk."

But it was talk that made sense to me. I said to her, "Who else would have killed Dillon?"

"I don't know. But you can't go believing rumors, Tuff! People always say bad things about anybody who's different."

Dammit, she made sense, too. Better sense than the kid with yellow teeth. I couldn't go out and swipe a shotgun just yet.

"You can't go accusing somebody when you don't have any proof," Monica said softly.

The way she looked at me, I realized she liked me. Maybe not the way she had liked Dillon, but she liked me some.

I muttered, "So what would you do?"

"If I was suspicious about somebody, I'd go to the cops."

"Hell, no." The cops didn't care. I felt myself starting to boil again and got up to leave before I went and showed her my nasty side. I didn't want to do that. Things were ugly enough already.

Anyway, I knew what I could do. I told her, "I'm going to have a talk with this mountain man." If I knocked long enough the guy had to let me in. "I'll just go out and talk to him."

"No, Tuff, don't!"

"Monica, it'll be okay."

"Tuff—"

But I had walked away.

First thing when I got home from school, I said, "Pen, can we go to Quarryville tonight? Talk to people?" I'd figure out how to get to Sid's Mountain once he said yes to Quarryville.

But he was way ahead of me. He said, "Tuff, listen, we have to go get you some decent clothes tonight, because the viewing's tomorrow."

I could tell he had it all planned, how he was going to keep me out of trouble. The nearest real mall was thirty miles away, and he would take his time getting there and back. He didn't want me to find out who killed Dillon. He just wanted me to leave it alone.

But how could I not go along with him? He had pulled off a funeral for Dillon, for God's sake. Now he wanted to get me a suit to wear to it. Not to mention he had saved my life. Not to mention I liked him, sometimes I damn near loved him, and he seemed to like me. I felt ashamed about the way I'd cursed at him the night before.

I felt dead tired.

"We can get supper someplace," Pen said. "You like Taco Bell?"

"Sure," I said. "Taco Bell sounds good."

It was funny, how the anger came and went. I could be cool awhile, a few hours, maybe even a day, but then all of a sudden it would hit like lightning out of nowhere, and I would be so mad I couldn't see. Though now that I look back I can tell I was never really without it, even when I thought I was cool, even when I was trying to sleep, because I needed it to keep me going. It was my friend, staying with me so I wouldn't be lonely, whispering in my mind all day and all night that I was going to find the guy who killed Dillon.

But it was like having a snake for a friend.

It could have turned on the wrong person. It could have turned on Pen.

"You like pizza better?" Pen asked. "Pizza Shack?"

"Fine. Either."

I was okay, I had it under control. I let Pen take me to Taco Bell. And I let him take me to the mall and buy me a suit and two dress shirts and a tie and some good shoes. He even bought me socks and a baseball jacket to wear to school. Each place we went he had to try different charge cards until he found one that was not quite maxed yet. This guy, up to his earlobes in debt, was spending money on me?

On our way out, he stopped and threw a quarter into the fountain. "Make a wish," he said.

I shook my head hard. My only wishes were about Dillon, and they hurt too bad.

Pen looked at me. "Sorry," he muttered. "Stupid thing to say."

I made it back to Pen's place okay, but that night, lying on the sofa, I hurt all over. I curled up with hurting. I wanted Dillon so bad—but no, goddammit, wanting was no use, wishing I had him back was no use. The only thing worth squat would be to blow away the guy who killed him.

Then the anger coiled like a blood-red rattle-snake and hissed loud enough to drown out the pain. I didn't need to curl up anymore. I lay there straight and still and very quietly tore apart a sofa pillow with my bare hands.

Kill. Kill the bastard who shot Dillon.

Thinking about it really helped. It got so I was hard like a knife lying there, sharp and wide awake, waiting. Around three in the morning, when I was sure Pen had to be sleeping like a log, I got up.

I soft-footed into Pen's bedroom and looked at him first, kind of saying good-bye, because I knew what I was about to do might turn him against me. I knew it was serious and I couldn't expect him to forgive me.

There he lay, on his back with his belly sticking up, snoring a little, just an ordinary-looking guy sleeping in his undershorts. Polka-dot ones. Skimpy little hairs catching the light around his navel. He had more peach fuzz down there than he did on his bald spot. His ears were stupid looking, kind of fat on top. I had only known him three days. Why should he matter so much to me? Just because he was my father? Where had he been for the past sixteen years?

66

Dillon mattered more. Dillon came first, before anybody else.

I eased out of there, being very careful not to make noise. I opened the door to the store little by little, then slipped in. It took me awhile to find the key to the drawer where Pen kept his gun, but like I said I was real, real calm, in a strange stone-angry way. I just kept quietly feeling around until there it was, hanging on its hook. Once I had it I unlocked the drawer, pulled out the pistol, checked to make sure it was loaded, and hefted it in my hand. The glass cuts still hurt me some, but I'd figured I could handle a gun, and I was right. I took a box of ammunition, just in case, and closed the drawer. I locked it again and put the key back where it belonged.

I was crazy. I mean, I didn't understand it then, but I was insane. Grief can do that to a person if they try to tough it out.

The gun felt heavy and chilly and good in my hand. Dangerous, powerful. I liked that feeling of power, like I was finally in control of something.

I took the gun back in to where I was supposed to be sleeping, closing the door to the store very quietly behind me. I found my new baseball jacket and zipped the pistol and ammo in a pocket and laid the jacket so the bulge wouldn't show. I put a blanket over the sofa pillow I had ripped up. Then I lay down on top of it and waited for morning.

I was going to go talk to the mountain man. Just talk to him, I kept telling myself, because that was what I had promised Monica. But I needed the gun in case he tried to hurt me, didn't I? In case he tried to kill me the way he had killed Dillon.

6

In the morning I got up, got my shower, changed the bandages on my face for smaller ones, got dressed for school, had breakfast with Pen, all real calm. Pen watched me over his coffee, the way he always did. "The viewing's at seven tonight," he said.

I just nodded, all the time knowing I wouldn't be there—I would be either on the run or in jail. That meant I wouldn't make it to the funeral tomorrow, either. Dillon was dead, and dead people don't care, I told myself. Or, if he was looking down from somewhere, he would understand. I felt bad, telling myself that, and now I understand why: The truth was, I was chicken. I couldn't face what I had to do, which was put Dillon in a grave. But at the time I just told myself it was more important to get the killer.

"You know your mother's going to be there," Pen said.

The bitch. I felt the anger coiling and

stinging inside me, hidden in my chest, as I nodded again.

"She's going to need you to stand by her. Can you do that?"

"I can do what I have to," I said, which was the next best thing to a whopping lie. I stood up. It was time for the school bus to come. "See ya," I told Pen, knowing maybe I wouldn't see him again, maybe he wouldn't want to let me in his house again once he found out what I had done. Anger helped keep my shoulders hard. I picked up my new jacket and slung it on as I went out the door. I didn't look back.

All the way to school, I could feel the gun riding in my pocket, heavy and solid and secret.

When the bus pulled up to the front of the building, I got off with the others. I even went in. But then I walked straight on through and went out the back doors and kept walking.

It was a hike to Sid's Mountain from school, but not as far as it would have been to walk all the way from Dam Shame. I could have saved myself the hike and some waiting by taking Pen's car in the night, but the cops would have been after me the minute he found out. This way I would have some time. Pen would think I was in school, and the school would think I was home getting ready for my brother's funeral. Nobody would know where I was or what I was doing. Afterward, they would find out—but I didn't care about afterward. I couldn't feel any real interest in what was left of my life.

I got to Sid's Mountain before noon. But then it took me awhile to find the cabin, coming at it from a different direction than I was used to, through all that rough country. Moving quietly in case anybody was around, I got there by following the rock formation till I saw a thread of smoke. Yeah, there was smoke coming out of the chimney again.

I stood behind the closest angle of rock, unzipped my pocket and pulled out my gun, checked again to be sure it was loaded, and put it back in my pocket, with the zipper open this time.

I went to the door and knocked.

No answer.

Knocked some more.

No answer.

There's something about being shut out, locked out, that drives me psycho. I started to swear, and I kicked the door, and for a minute I decided I was going to break it down the way the cops do on TV. But then I got a little sense and went around the place to look at the windows instead. And for crying out loud, one of them was propped open. Not even a screen in it.

I swung myself up and bellied through the opening, already knowing that nobody was home. If the mountain man was there, I would have had a rifle barrel poked in my face by then.

Just the same, I looked around real careful when I got inside. The place was all one room. Not even a john. The guy must go in the woods someplace. No running water—covered buckets instead, and plastic milk jugs—probably brought the water in from a spring. A wood stove served for heat and cooking—there was a little fire going in it right now. There was a cot, a hickory chair, and a square table. I saw rabbit skins and some other kinds of skins stretched on boards that leaned against the walls. There wasn't much else to look at.

I sat in the chair, took out my gun and held it in my lap, and waited.

Hours went past, I'm not sure how many. I didn't have a watch.

Then—I never heard him coming, but the door opened and there he was.

We both jumped and went, "Aaaaa!"

He'd startled me as bad as I'd startled him, and I'd been expecting him—but knock me silly, he was worse than I would have thought even from hearing kids talk about him. The stink, for one thing—I should have smelled him coming, even if I didn't hear him—and the rags letting big bony patches of him show through. And the beard hanging down him the way brown hairy stuff hangs down a tree sometimes. And the way he was holding a bloody hunk of meat in his hand, and the freaky eyes staring out of all that beard. His eyes scooted from my face to my gun to my face again, wild and scared.

I was glad I had the pistol, but I didn't lift it or point it at him. He didn't have any weapon that I could see—maybe there was a hunting knife on him somewhere, but he was nowhere near close enough to me to use it, and his hunting rifle was hanging on the wall behind me. He was across the room from it and from me.

No shotgun.

Maybe he had owned a shotgun and it was missing. Maybe he had wired it to a tree. Maybe the cops had it now.

I said, "Hi. Uh, I'm Shawn. Shawn Lacey."

He dropped the meat on the floor and didn't answer.

"What's your name?"

His eyes went even crazier, and he didn't say a word.

I said, "Okay, then I'll call you Mountain Man. That's what everybody calls you, right?" No answer. "Listen, I just want to talk to you about something. It's about my brother Dillon." The mountain man was staring like a gonzo person, and I kept making what I said simpler and simpler, because I couldn't tell how much he understood. "He got killed, Dillon got killed. Up the mountain. Up above the rocks, on the dirt road. Somebody put up a shotgun wired to go off. He ran into the string and got killed. You know about that?"

He stared.

I asked again, "You know about that?"

His beard moved. He was nodding.

"You do?" My heart pounded with excitement, I was so sure he could tell me something. I stood up with the gun in my hand hanging down by my side. He took a step back from me, jamming himself against the closed door. "Listen," I told him, "I just want to talk. I need to know who did it. Can you talk to me? Can you tell me who did it?"

His mouth came open and closed again, soft and round, like a fish drowning. He had bad teeth, long and brown. He was stepping on the meat he had been carrying. His hands were red with blood.

I asked him, "Did *you* have anything to do with it?"

Then his face changed. And when I saw it, when I saw the guilt in his face, the rage hit like—forget lightning, it was worse. Wildfire. A firestorm.

I started to shake with fury. My hand came up, shaking, and pointed the gun at him, because his face was curled up with guilt and I knew, I just knew, he had done it. The son of a bitch had killed my brother. He had killed Dillon.

I whispered, "You." I was so crazy mad my voice wasn't working right. I couldn't even curse him properly. "You bastard." And I didn't have a shotgun to kill him with. But I could not wait. The pistol was the next best thing. Bullets would make holes and he would bleed—it was good enough. I panted at him, "Out the door. Move!"

His face was curled up with terror now, and he stumbled outside.

I wanted to kill him where Dillon had died.

If I had been thinking, I would not have tried it, because once we got in the woods he could have made a run for it. But I wasn't thinking—I was nuts. I headed him up the mountain and stayed close behind him, and he didn't try to get away. It was like he thought he deserved what he was going to get.

When we got there, the yellow police line was gone. I took him right to where it had happened, beside the tree with the wire scars on it, and I stopped him there and made him turn around and face me. It was late in the day and the shadows were long. "Why?" I asked him, with my gun pointing at his heart.

He was shaking and panting and making small whimpering noises deep in his throat. They made me angrier.

"I want to know why you did it!" I yelled at him. "Why?"

No answer.

"Goddammit. Didn't you even do it for a *reason*?"

He shook his head. I wanted to kill him that moment. Blow him away. But I had to wait, I had to do this right.

"Kneel," I told him.

He didn't move. He was looking past me.

By my side a quiet voice said, "Shawn, stop. You don't know he did anything."

Penrose Leppo.

Where the hell did he come from? I jumped about three feet sideward, away from him. "Get out of here!" I screamed at him.

Real flat, he said, "Why? You thinking of doing something wrong?"

I kept the gun up, aimed at the mountain man. I was so mad I could barely talk. "Just go away."

"Sure, and let you ruin your life. Shoot an innocent man."

"He's not innocent! He—killed . . ." I couldn't say it. My gun hand was throbbing, pounding like my heart. I wanted to pull the trigger.

Pen stood there solid and quiet and said, "You think he killed Dillon? Can you prove anything?"

"I know he did it! He's guilty as hell. Look at him!"

Pen said, "You don't know a thing. You don't even know who this is, but I do. His name is Al Quigg, and he was a high school classmate of mine. Right, Quiggie?"

The guy opened his mouth and struggled

with air a minute. "P-P-P-Penrose," he said. "H-how you b-b-been?"

Pen smiled at him and nodded and kept talking to me. "Quiggie was on the basketball team," he said. "He was a real sports star. All the girls liked him back then, before he got so shaggy. And—this is something you might want to consider—it's very possible he is your father. I sure as hell know I am not."

I wouldn't have thought anything could hit me harder than the firestorm of anger taking me over, but that did. It hit like a brick wall landing on my chest. I could barely breathe. The gun sagged down to my side. I swung around and gawked at Pen, but I couldn't talk.

He said very quiet, "Your ma and I never— I was never her boyfriend, Shawn. But Quiggie was. Isn't that true, Quiggie? You remember Candy Lacey?"

I swear to God he smiled. "C-C-Candy," he said. "Oh yeah."

"Those babies she had when she was still a kid, one of them could have been yours?"

"M-maybe. I d-d-dunno, I was in p-p-p-prison—"

"But they could have been."

"M-m-mine? B-b-but sh-she don't know that. Sh-she don't know who their f-f-fathers was. Sh-she had l-l-lots of d-d-d-different—"

"Shut up!" I screamed at him. I couldn't stand listening to him sputter and stutter. I couldn't stand hearing what he was saying. I wanted to blow him away. I brought the pistol up and took aim at him.

"Okay, Tuff stuff," Pen said to me, sounding tired and bored. "I'm not trying to stop you. You want to be a murderer? Go ahead, do it if you're going to."

And he stood there.

And Quiggie stood there whimpering in his throat again, and I stood there with the gun shaking in my hand.

And I couldn't do it.

It wasn't because Pen was watching or because I knew I would go to jail, maybe even get a death sentence. I honest to God didn't care what happened to me. And it wasn't because this twitchy, stuttering, stinky weirdo, Al Quigg, might have been my father. I couldn't really believe that. And it wasn't because I had no proof he did anything to Dillon. I still thought he was the one.

It was just that—I couldn't kill him.

I was still red-hot blind with rage and pain, more now than ever, since Pen was talking to me so hard and cold, since he said he was not my father. And I still wanted to kill the mountain man. But something in me would not let me pull the trigger. I'd never really known before, but—I wasn't the kind of person who could kill people, not even for Dillon. He had raised me too good. I just was not a killer.

I guess Pen knew.

It was no use standing there. I could stand there all day, pointing the gun at the mountain man, my hand shaking, and not get anywhere. I couldn't hurt him. I had to let him go.

I closed my eyes and let my arm ease down to my side.

There was a loud bang. At the same time something hit me, knocking me to the ground.

Somewhere close by a gun had gone off, and it wasn't mine.

7

Another few shots whistled over us as I lay there facedown in the dirt with Pen on top of me. It wasn't a bullet that had hit me. It was him, knocking me down to save my life. Again.

Somebody was shooting at us, and it sure as hell was not Al Quigg, the mountain man, because there he was lying right beside me, whimpering to himself.

"Shawn, the pistol," Pen said in my ear. "Quick, give me the gun!"

I slipped it to him and grabbed the extra ammo out of my pocket and gave him that, too. "Stay flat on the ground," he said. "Get behind a tree or something." Then he rolled off me and did the opposite himself, getting up enough to run bent over toward the nearest rock. About three shots cracked at once—it was more than one person shooting at us. Pen landed on his gut, and I panicked, I thought he was hit.

"Pen!"

God, no, if I lost him, too, I would die—but he swiveled around and motioned at me to get down. He was okay, it was just that he had dived for cover. He had a quick look past the side of his rock, poked his pistol out, and pulled off three shots.

I don't think he hit anything. They shot back at him and chips of rock flew up where the bullets hit. Pen reached up and squeezed off a few more shots, but there's not much a guy with a handgun can do against goons with rifles. All Pen was doing was keeping them busy, drawing their attention away from Quiggie and me while we crawled behind a couple of trees.

"G-G-Green Beret," Quiggie stuttered to me proudly. "P-P-P-Pen was."

God. My little pudgy father was a Green Beret?

Only—he said he wasn't my father.

I couldn't answer Quiggie or show that I heard what he said. I was so shot to hell, I couldn't talk. I should have been doing something to help Pen, but I couldn't think what. Too—scared, yeah, but mostly I didn't care if I died. When was I ever going to stop hurting? Dillon was dead, and my mother didn't care, and my father—I couldn't bear to think about it.

I never want to feel like that again, so flattened. The guns cracked and popped, and I just lay there a few feet from where Dillon had been killed, waiting for it to be over.

"Police!" blared a megaphone voice out of nowhere. "Throw down your weapons!"

Pen dropped his. The other guys did not. They shot at the cops. The cops returned fire. Now there were bullets flying over us from a different angle than before. Quiggie gave up whimpering and just plain wailed. I grabbed him by the waist and pulled him closer to me, where he had more shelter. God, he stank like a hound dog that's been eating roadkill, and he kept howling like one, too.

I put my head down and waited some more, just hanging on. Don't ask me how long it took, but after a while the gunfire moved off up the mountain somewhere, and neither of us had been hit. Pen, either—I could see him sitting up, and he looked okay.

Quiggie stopped his noise, staggered up, and made a run for it, scuttling to his cabin. What a day for him. Shot at, kidnapped by me— God, I was a jerk. I closed my eyes and lay where I was.

"I thought I told you to stay the hell away from here!" somebody yelled, standing over me. Detective Mohatt. I recognized his voice, but I didn't move or open my eyes or look up at him.

"He has a right to be here." The quiet voice was Pen's. "It's state land."

"Somebody seems to think it's a shooting range, in case you haven't noticed, Leppo. Get him out of here." Mohatt stomped off.

Pen hunkered down beside me. "Tuff, come on." His hands were gentle on my shoulders.

I started crying.

I couldn't help it. There was nothing else to do. I clenched my fists against the earth but anger was no use—I couldn't kill Quiggie or anybody else, all I was left with was the god-damn awful pain and no place to go with it. Dillon, my brother—I wanted him so bad, and there was not a frigging thing I could do that would ever bring him back. No miracles for me. No father could make it all right, either, even if I knew who my father was, which I did not know and I never would.

I shook all over with sobbing. Pen sat down on the ground beside me and pulled me up into his arms so that I was crying against his chest instead of lying with my face in the dirt.

He held me and cradled my head with his hands and didn't try to say anything, just hugged me. I should have been embarrassed, I guess, with him holding me like a baby, but I was too far gone. Anyway, there was something about Pen.

"We've got to get you out of here," he muttered finally, and his voice was husky. I sat up and saw there were tears on his face, too.

The next few hours were pretty blurry. I couldn't stop crying, but it was dusk and Pen had to get me off Sid's Mountain before night fell or Mohatt came back, or the guys with the guns. I just barely remember walking down, then being in the car with him, pressing my face against the window glass, trying to stop the tears. Pen took me home—to his place, I mean—and cleaned me up, and I guess I shouldn't say this but when the sobbing kept coming back he gave me a shot of whiskey. He didn't try to talk to me or anything, he knew I couldn't take it, but I still kept coming apart. It was late by the time I got even halfway calmed down, too late to go to the viewing.

Late, and somebody rapped on the door. Pen went and opened it.

"Saw your light was still on," grumped a

voice I knew. Detective Mohatt came in, looking rumpled and tired.

"Listen up, Shawn," he snapped at me, getting ready to do some more yelling. But then
he looked at me, and his face changed, and so
did his voice. "You okay?"

I'd mostly quit crying by then, finally, but I
guess my face was a mess, and I didn't care.
Who cared what Mohatt thought? I looked
straight at him, and no, I wasn't okay. "I will
be," I said. Someday. Maybe.

"You look like hell," Mohatt said.

I shook my head, tired of me. "Did you get
them?" All I wanted from Mohatt was one
thing: Dillon's killer in handcuffs. I wanted to
know who it was and why he did it. I wanted
to look at him through jail bars and know who
to hate. I wanted to see if he could face me.

"No, goddammit." Mohatt sat down at Pen's
table. Sitting down like that, he didn't seem
like such a bad guy. More like a guy who drank
too much coffee. Wired all the time.

"We think they're a small-time drug gang,"
he said. "We found some places up there
where they planted something, probably mari-
juana. Gangs do that sometimes, find a piece
of public land and move in and take over. Try
to scare off anybody who comes around."

String a trap. Don't care who they hurt or kill. Don't care if they kill Dillon. My brother.

Right then it seemed to me, of all the bad things in the world, the worst thing was that some people just didn't care.

"They're holed up in the rocks somewhere," Mohatt said. "That mountain is like a playground to them. They're laughing at us."

I burst out at him, "Can't you—"

All of a sudden Mohatt was steamed. He cut me off. "Son, don't try to tell me what to do. I know what I can and can't do. I can't nab anybody until I know who they are and where to find them. Do you know who they are? Did you see them?"

No, dammit. I shook my head.

"Leppo?"

Pen came and sat down with us. "Nope. All I saw was rifle barrels."

"Then we're screwed. For now. I'm gonna go home and get a little sleep." Mohatt got up, but then he just stood there looking at me. "Listen, Tuff," he said, "I want these guys as much as you do."

Not possible. I said nothing, but I looked back at him.

He sighed, and his voice went quiet. "You know I told you to stay away from that mountain," he said. "My ulcer can't stand this kind of crap. Next it'll be you full of holes, and I'll be standing over you studying the blood splatters and the puke and the dirt under your fingernails. You want that?"

I didn't know what to say. Pen stood beside me as if to protect me, but Mohatt didn't make me answer. "Think about it," he said. "God knows I do." Then he turned and headed out.

"Hungry?" Pen asked. I was sitting at his kitchen table sometime after midnight. It was like a replay of that first night, when I broke in.

I shook my head.

He sat down next to me and started to work on my face. I had melted the bandages off it pretty good, crying, and he had to tape the splint back on my nose now that I was finally done. "How do you feel?"

"Weird." I felt light and hollow, like an eggshell with no stuffing. "There's a hole in me that's bigger than I am."

He nodded like he knew. "That's the way I felt after my wife died."

"How long does it last?" It was a scary feeling. Lonesome.

"Awhile."

He finished taping the splint on my nose and put antiseptic on some cuts on my face that had opened. He said, "You'll get over it when it's time."

He pushed the first-aid box away. We sat there.

"You sure you're not hungry?"

I shook my head. If he wasn't even my father, why was he so damn good to me? I blurted out, "You're not pissed at me?"

That made him smile. "Should I be?"

"I stole your gun."

It was back in the drawer, and the key was in his pocket. But now he took the key out of his pocket and hung it on the wall where I could see it. He said, real quiet, "Well, it's not going to happen again, is it? You know now that it won't do any good."

I said, "You wouldn't have let me shoot him, would you?" If he was fast enough to snag a copperhead, he was fast enough to knock a gun out of my hand when I went to pull the trigger.

He gave me half a smile, admitting it. "But I won't always be around," he said.

"And you're just going to leave that there?"

"Yes."

I couldn't figure him out. We sat there some more.

He said, "I've been too worried about you to get mad at you."

I begged him, "You sure you're not my father?" And if I was made of eggshell, I had just cracked open. I thought I was worn out enough to talk about things now, but I wasn't. My voice started to come apart. I couldn't look at him.

He reached over and put his hands on my shoulders. I could almost feel him thinking. Then he said, very softly, "Tuff, what is a father? You tell me. Is it the guy who gets your mom pregnant?"

I didn't answer. I still couldn't look at him.

He said, "Tuff, listen. I loved your mother." Just like that, like saying water is wet. "She was . . ." He tried to think of a way to put it. "She was, you know the song, she was like the wind. The wildest, most beautiful, laugh-at-the-devil thing I had ever seen. But she collected big, good-looking men. She didn't want a little fat boy like me."

That made me look at him. "You're not fat!"

"Sure, I'm not. Tell me another." He grinned at me, but then he stopped grinning. "She did care about me some," he said. "That's why she told me to stop hanging around, to go take a hike. She told me she was poison, she would make me miserable, she wanted me to be happy, I should get the hell out while I could."

I hated her for his sake. "And meanwhile she was banging every guy in three counties."

"She did it with whoever she wanted, Tuff. She was a rebel."

God, he still . . . "But she told you to get lost."

"That's right."

I didn't want to start crying again. My ribs wouldn't take it. I closed my eyes.

Pen said in that no-fuss way of his, "Tuff, listen, if a father to you is a specific guy who had sex with your mom, then I think you're out of luck. But if a father is a guy who—who cares about you. . . ."

His voice wasn't no-fuss now. He was having trouble saying this. I opened my eyes and stared at him.

He tried it again. "If a father is a guy who cares about you, I think I qualify." His voice would not behave for him. "Look, Shawn, son, I—I've been happy, I've had a lot of good things in my life, but I never had a kid. If you—listen, money's not that much of a problem, I can get a job. We can close the store, make it into a room for you—"

I was barely breathing.

"What I mean is, if it's okay with your mom—and you want to stay here with me—"

I don't remember what I said. Maybe I didn't say anything. Probably not, because I didn't need to. I just leaned forward a little and put my arms around him, and we hugged each other like crazy.

8

That night I slept like a baby from the minute I finally lay down. I don't remember moving or having a dream. I don't remember a thing until Pen woke me up close to noon the next day.

"Hey, Pa!" I stretched out my hand to him, grinning. I felt a little drunk.

"Morning, Son." He took my hand and shook it like we had reached an agreement. But he was a lot more sober than I was, and he was dressed in a suit and tie.

Oh, my Christ. We had to go to a funeral today. Dillon's funeral.

It hit me like a club, and for a minute I couldn't move. Pen must have seen it happen. He said softly, "Shawn, you'll be okay. Whoever tagged you 'Tuff' got it right. You can do what you have to do."

I nodded and got myself in gear enough to sit up. Shower, I told myself. Get dressed.

"You want something to eat?" Pen asked. "I

can fix you some pancakes, or a sandwich."

The thought of food made my stomach flip. I shook my head.

"Tuff, when's the last time you ate? Yesterday morning?"

"I guess." I stood up. "I'll eat afterward, Pen, I promise." I was afraid I would puke or something.

In the shower I felt like I was going to faint, I was so dizzy. When I got dressed, Pen had to take care of my tie for me. I kept fumbling with the knot like I'd never done one before. Well, I hadn't, or not very often. Pen stood behind me and reached over my shoulders and tied the thing for me. Then he turned me around and stepped back to have a look.

"You look good," he said.

I did look okay, I guess. It was the best suit I had ever owned. Actually, it was the first suit I had ever owned. Dillon would have teased me. *Stud muffin*, he would have called me. *Hey, Tuff, you studly dude, you. When you gonna do it, Tuff? When you gonna find you a girl?*

"My God, you're smiling," Pen said.

"I'm light-headed," I told him.

"You sure you can't eat?"

"No way."

We got in the car. He had shined it up a little while I was asleep. He drove slow, like it was Sunday. We didn't say anything most of the way there, but Pen was thinking. I could see him scowling at the windshield.

"Listen, Tuff," he said. Here it came. "Why do you figure your mother told you I was your father?"

Now that I had gotten some sleep and my mind was starting to function for a change, I had been thinking about that, too. I said, "Because she wishes it was true." He was probably the only one who had ever really loved her.

His mouth dropped open and he took his foot off the gas. Then he shook his head. "Nah," he said.

I had a feeling I was right, but I asked him, "Well, why do you think she did it?"

"Because she knew you would go to me, and she knew I would take you in. See, Candy knows I have this idea of trying to be a hero." He rolled his eyes, making fun of himself. "She knew I would want to help you."

Help, hell. He had saved me. Saved my life. In more ways than one.

He said quietly, "See, Shawn, she cared what happened to you. She cares about you more than you think. Give her some credit, okay?"

Mom was the one who had snapped the picture of me and Dillon on that bike, and she'd had to borrow the camera to do it, and find money to pay for film. She never said much or even smiled much, but she did things. She had scrounged me a fishing knife because she knew I wanted one. Then kind of threw it at me so I wouldn't say thank you. Mom was tough, but she—her life was tougher.

I looked out the window so Pen wouldn't see my face.

"Okay, Tuff?"

I nodded.

He drove awhile, then he said, "She's not the only one who cares, either. People in general care about you more than you want to notice. Mohatt—he cares, even though he'd never admit it. And that girl Monica—you like her? She really likes you."

I jerked my head around to gawk at him. "When did you meet Monica?"

"Yesterday. She came to the store looking for you to see how you were doing because you hadn't been in school."

Which was news to him.

"In other words, she saved your ass."

"You saved my ass," I told him.

"Only because she was smart enough to figure out where you had gone and tell me. And she called the cops, or we would both be ventilated."

"Monica did all that?"

"Yep."

But why the hell would she? I sat there wondering. She seemed to kind of like me—but why? Because I had been going around with my emotions hanging out? Because I liked her?

It startled me silly, thinking that, because I didn't realize till right then how much I really liked Monica, and it was crazy, because she wasn't the kind— She wasn't a girl like the one I was chasing—I didn't even remember her name—before Dillon died. Monica wasn't like the kind of girl Dillon would have picked for me at all. She didn't strut and wiggle her butt and she didn't have raccoon eyes and pouty lips and she didn't—she wasn't hot, you know? But there was something—

"Yeppers." Pen glanced over at me with his eyebrows twitching, getting set to tease. "You might want to be nice to Monica," he said. "I know that's going to be a serious effort for a stud like you."

"I'll force myself," I told him.

I wondered about this love thing between men and women. Did my mother ever really have love? Did Dillon ever have love, or did he just have fun?

Dillon, you idiot. I had to close my eyes. He would not have given Monica a second glance, and I—I had to try not to think about it anymore, how much he had missed out on. I would have wanted everything good for him if he had hung around, but the jerk, he had to go and die.

When we drove up to the funeral home, there were people everywhere. What was going on? I mean, was some important person going to be there or something?

Then some of them came up to me when I got out of the car, and I realized a lot of them were kids from school. Kids who knew Dillon, kids who knew me, kids he'd played ball with. And some of them were people he'd worked with. And some of them were neighbors, river people. They weren't there to see somebody important—they were there for Dillon. I never knew so many people cared about him.

"My most sincere condolences, young man,"

some old lady said to me while Pen parked the car.

"What a pisser, huh, Tuff?" some kid said. Most of them were standing around like they didn't know what to say. I didn't know what to say, either.

"Shawn? The family is inside." Some big guy in a three-piece gray suit beckoned to me.

"Wait." I was looking for somebody, and then I saw her. "Monica!" She was wearing a baggy dark dress and standing way in back of everybody. I pushed through the crowd to get to her. "Monica."

"Tuff, you look nice," she told me with a little smile. "Could use a haircut, but hey. A person can't have everything."

I couldn't believe it, she almost made me laugh. "Come sit with me?" I asked her. "Please."

She stopped smiling and looking worried. "Tuff, I can't do that! I'm not family. I barely knew Dillon."

"Dillon's not asking you," I told her. "I'm asking you." I reached out toward her, and I guess she understood: I needed her to hold my hand. She nodded and put her hand into mine, and I held on tight.

There were six bawling big-hair girls hanging around outside the doors. Monica and I walked past them and slipped inside.

There were people everywhere in there, too, standing around or sitting in rows of chairs. And flowers—there were bunches of flowers everywhere. Flowers from schoolteachers, flowers from the people at the car wash, flowers from people Dillon mowed lawns for, flowers from, I swear to God, the hairy-chin woman at the boat rental place. Flowers from the old guy who used to take us deer hunting out of season before his arthritis got too bad. Flowers from people we had met on the river. Flowers from people we didn't even know.

Pen was in there. He smiled at me and gave me the thumbs-up and stayed where he was, pressed against the back wall, near the door.

The coffin was up front.

"Okay," I whispered to myself or Monica, and we walked slowly up there.

People moved out of our way and gave us a half circle of space. And silence. It was so quiet. All those people in the room and barely any noise.

Dillon was the quietest of all.

I stood there and looked at him, at my

brother Dillon—it was him lying there in the coffin, yet it was not him. Just his body. They had him dressed up in a suit, with a tie, and a collar high enough to hide the buckshot holes. They had him lying straight, and all pink colored, with lipstick on him, for God's sake, and his hair slicked back. It was him, yet it was a stranger, an alien. I touched his face, and he was like plastic. His eyes were closed, but he was not sleeping. I couldn't wake him up and say, Hey, let's go down to the river. He had nothing to do with me anymore.

I don't think I really understood till then what *dead* meant, and I could barely stand it. I hung on to Monica's hand and tears ran down my face. The gray-suit guy walked over from somewhere and offered me a hankie, but I didn't want it from him. He reminded me of a pimp or something.

"Just a minute," I said to him, like he was going to take Dillon away, and I reached into that damn coffin and mussed up Dillon's hair. At least his hair could look normal. It was stiff, they had sprayed it or something, but I fixed that. I mussed it up good, like it was blowing in the wind, going fast up a mountain.

That was the last I ever saw him. I went and

sat down next to my mother, and they closed the coffin.

Mom looked sober and old. She had makeup on, and her hair was curled like a girl's, but her face was full of lines that pulled it down. I had never noticed them before.

"You okay?" I asked her.

She nodded.

"You got a Kleenex?" I needed one. Should have taken the damn hankie.

Mom shook her head. I should have known better than to ask. She never had a Kleenex, even when I was a little kid. She was not that kind of mom.

"Monica?" She was sitting next to me on the other side, and I was still hanging on to her hand. "You got a Kleenex?"

"Nuh-uh. Sorry."

"What is it with you women?" I complained. "Aren't you supposed to always carry big purses full of Kleenex and stuff?"

"Not this woman." She said it with that soft little smile of hers. I loved her smile.

"Tuff," Mom said. I turned back to her, and she had borrowed a tissue from somebody for me. Well, not borrowed. When I finished using it I felt pretty sure they didn't want it back.

Mom said to me, "The kids keep asking where Dillon is." She sounded very tired. "They don't understand. They saw him at the viewing last night, but they still don't understand."

I saw them heading across the room toward us, dodging between chairs and peoples' legs, the oldest one, Tyler, herding the two middle ones, Julie and Eve. Mom must have left the two littlest ones with their father, which was probably a good idea. Three was enough. Mom was in no shape to get through Dillon's funeral if she had to handle five squirmy kids.

The brats looked nice. Mom had found the girls dresses somewhere, and Tyler had on a sport coat and bow tie. His collie-blond hair shagged over the collar. His jaw stuck out. He looked like one tough little dude.

"They've been asking where you are, too," Mom said. "Are you coming back?" No tears or anything, yet something about the way she said it touched my heart.

I looked at her. She didn't look like such a bad deal of a mom. Instead of answering her question I asked her, "Why did you tell me Pen is my father?"

"Huh?" She blinked at me. "I said that?"

"Yes, you did. How come?"

"Hell, how would I know, honey? I was drunk. I don't remember."

Probably she didn't remember what she said about Dillon being dead, either. Probably at the time she just couldn't face it. I knew the feeling.

I knew I had to forgive her.

I told her, "Well, the funny thing is, Pen *is* my father now."

"No, he isn't."

"Yes, he is. He's my pa."

Then she started to understand, and she smiled, and the smile lifted up her face and took away some of the lines.

Tyler stood in front of me, scowling. "You're in my seat," he said.

"Oh. Well, c'mere." I reached out for him. I don't know what made me do it, but I pulled him over and sat him on my lap. He stiffened a minute—being six, he was a little bit old for lap sitting. But it was a rough day, so I guess he figured he could make an exception. He relaxed some and leaned against me, very still.

He was my half brother. So was Dillon, probably—not my full brother, only a half brother, judging from what I knew now. But it didn't have to matter. Pen wasn't really my pa at all, and it didn't matter.

Monica was no relation to anybody, but there were little Eve and Julie both sitting in her lap, snuggled against her.

"Are you coming home with us?" Tyler asked, low, not looking at me.

I looked at Mom. She looked back at me and said to Tyler, not quite steadily, "We have to think what's best for Shawn. You know him and your pa don't always get along."

I said to both of them, "I can visit you."

"You damn well better. Soon," Mom said. "You've got a stack of sympathy cards this high." She showed me with her hands. "Everybody's driving me crazy, asking about you."

"I'll come Saturday," I promised her. I joggled Tyler to make him look at me. "Hey," I told him, "you want me to, I'll take you fishing."

9

I got through the funeral somehow, between holding Monica's hand and feeling Tyler sitting there warm against my chest. Those two helped more than God, no matter what the preacher said. I didn't listen to the preacher much, because he was trying to talk about Dillon and he didn't even know him. He didn't know anything about Dillon or about me, so I tuned him out. Mostly I sat there and tried to think whether I believed in life after death and all that. Like, would I meet up with Dillon again? I kind of wanted to believe it, but the way people talked about heaven, it sounded like a stupid fairy tale, not like any place Dillon would want to hang around. Play a harp in drag, for God's sake? Screw that. Dillon would want to be someplace with motorcycles and danger and fun, not a country-club heaven where they wouldn't want to let in long-hair kids like him and me anyway.

But maybe people didn't know. I mean, they

try to tell you about heaven and hell, but how can anybody really know? Maybe there could be a different kind of meet-again for Dillon and me.

I wanted to believe in something. Not God, exactly, not if God took Dillon away from me. But something.

The drive to the cemetery wasn't too bad. Pen drove Monica and the kids. Mom wanted me to come with her in the undertaker's car, and I did.

I got through the graveside service okay. The hardest part was when it was actually time to leave. The preacher said Amen, go in peace, but nobody went. All of us under the tent just sat there, and nobody said a word, and nobody could seem to turn away and go. The silence echoed, it was so quiet. Every little sound, people breathing, it echoed back from the grave like from a place so far away I can't describe it. Like from outer space. Like from a black hole. If the world ends I think it might do it that quietly, I think it might echo that way.

Mom started to cry.

I put my arm around her, and she leaned against me for a minute. But then she sat up straight and muttered, "C'mon," and stood up and led us all out of there. She was tough, and she was right. It was time. It was over.

Out in the sunshine, I held on tight to Monica's hand, breathed deep, and looked around. The world was still there after all, and people—in a funny, choked-up way it helped, having people there. Pen was standing right by my side. Neighbors stood around, river people. Even the cops were there. Even Detective Mohatt.

And somebody I wouldn't have expected, way off at the edge of the crowd, trying not to be noticed.

I let go of Monica's hand and hurried over to him. I guess I had been kind of in a daze, or I would have seen him before. Or maybe he had been hiding from me. When he saw me coming he got shy and started to turn away, but I called to him, "Mr. Quigg!"

I guess hardly anybody ever called him that. He got goggle-eyed and stood where he was while I walked up to him. He was in a weird polyester outfit with wide pants—probably that suit was older than I was. I wondered what he'd gone through to get it. And he had washed, too. And hiked down from his mountain. It'd taken a lot for him to be there.

"Listen, I'm really sorry," I told him.

"D-D-Dillon," he said.

I wasn't sure what he meant. He was sorry about Dillon? I was sorry about Dillon? I was Dillon? I said, "I'm Shawn. What I mean is, I was a real jerk, okay? Threatening you and accusing you and everything. I was stupid, okay? I'm sorry I bothered you."

Quiggie stretched one of his scrawny hands out toward me and said, "I s-s-saw them. I sh-sh-should have done s-s-something."

He had that guilty look on his face again, like he'd got when I asked him if he had anything to do with Dillon getting killed. This time, instead of pointing a gun at him, I figured maybe I better just listen.

I said, "You saw something?"

"I s-s-saw them p-p-p-put it up. I sh-sh-should have t-t-t-told them not to. I sh-should have m-m-m-made them take it down."

"You saw people putting up the shotgun?"

He nodded.

"*Who?*"

Too loud. He shrank back from me and sputtered and couldn't talk. I had to control myself.

I said more softly, "They were loaded for bear, right?"

Nod.

I could tell why he hadn't done anything about it. He was scared. Goddamn him, he could have saved my brother—

No, he couldn't. He was Quiggie. A misfit squatting on state land. A poor old lonesome loony, one oar out of the water, shingles loose on his roof, not hitting the head pin, several fries short of a Happy Meal. No way I could really expect him to do anything. It was amazing enough that he had come to Dillon's funeral.

I told him, "It's not your fault." He wasn't the one who had wired the shotgun up to the tree.

"The sons of bitches want to take over." Now that Quiggie was more mad than scared, he could talk okay. "They don't want nobody on that mountain but them. I hide, I hide from them all the time."

"Who? Who are they?"

"B-b-b-bad people."

Dammit, I knew that. "I mean, like, do you know their names?"

Quiggie shook his head.

"Are they still there? Do you know where they live?"

He nodded.

Thinking about it, I felt my chest go tight and my heart start pounding. Quiggie had a rifle. He was such a wimp, I knew I could boss him, he would do whatever I said. He could lead me to them. We could go up on the mountain and blow these guys away.

Then I blew my breath out and let it go. I had been through this before, and it was no damn good. Hating was no use. Killing was no use. Dillon was still lying in the ground.

I told Quiggie, "C'mon." I looked around for Detective Mohatt. "We have to tell the cops."

"N-n-no police!" Quiggie got his wild-eyed scared look and started to back away. "They-they-they'll run me off."

"Mr. Quigg, please." That stopped him. Being a Mister seemed to do something for him. "You feel bad because Dillon died—listen, this is one way to make up for it. Help nail the bastards that did it."

"They-they-they'll kill me."

Pen walked up. He must have been watching for a while and listening in, because he said, "I won't let them hurt you, Al."

He meant it, too. That's the kind of guy he is.

And it worked. Because Penrose G. Leppo had promised to protect him, Albert Quigg went and stuttered at Detective Mohatt and told him all about it.

"Three of them?" Mohatt asked.

"Yu-yu-yup."

Mohatt had his notebook out. "And you can describe them?"

Quiggie gave pretty good descriptions. "I s-s-s-seen them lots of times." He stood up taller and looked kind of proud. "I wa-wa-watch them. I'm g-g-g-good in the woods."

"You think you know where they are right now? Can you lead me to them? Me and some officers."

"S-s-sure I can." The look on Quiggie's face, he could have been a Green Beret. Pen stood beside me, watching and smiling.

"Then let's go." They started off. But then Mohatt turned and looked back at me. "Shawn," he said, "we'll get them, even if it's only for dealing. But with Mr. Quigg's testimony, I'm hoping to stick them with murder. And conspiracy."

I nodded.

"What about you? Will you testify?"

I gave him a look. "Hell, yes. I want them to rot in jail."

"So do I, son." It sounded like he and I actually agreed about something. "So do I."

———

Pen drove me back to the trailer because Mom needed me. Monica had to get home, so we dropped her off at her place. All the way there she sat between Pen and me, and even though I was holding her hand, I couldn't think of a damn thing to say. When I got out of the car to let her out, it was even worse. I felt terrified. She looked terrified.

Then she took my head in her hands and kissed me.

Just a little soft kiss on my splinted-up nose, of all places, where I couldn't even feel it. Except I did feel it, like an earthquake. Clear to my bones. Maybe it was because I hadn't eaten, but I got so dizzy I could barely breathe.

"See ya, Tuff," she whispered, and she kind of ran. I must have blipped out for a minute. Next thing I noticed, I was back in the car, it was heading down the road, and Pen was keeping his eyes on the road but he was grinning like an idiot.

"Oh, shut up," I told him.

"I didn't say a word!"

"You know what I mean."

He had his face mostly under control by the time we got to the trailer. Then I didn't see him awhile because he stayed outside. No room inside. Even less than usual, because the place was stuffed full of neighbors and food. People kept bringing food. Mom wedged me into a kitchen corner somehow and told me to get busy and eat, and I did. Ham on potato rolls, macaroni salad, sweet pickles, Jell-O, Nilla wafers. After a while I even got hungry. And the food even tasted good. That was the first time it made sense to me, that people would get together and eat after a funeral.

Mom's old man was there. He mumbled something to me about being sorry, and then he stayed away.

Later people started leaving, and Mom started drinking. Pen and I got out of there while she was still sober enough to hug me and send stuff home with me.

In the car I lay back and closed my eyes.

"How do you feel?" Pen asked.

I just felt really tired. "Sliced kind of thin." Like the chipped ham.

"Did you eat?"

"Yeah."

"Enough?"

"Yeah."

"How's your gut?"

"Okay." It only hurt a little.

Back at his place I changed into old clothes and hung up my suit. I looked at the stuff Mom had given me. Sympathy cards. Dillon's shirts and Harley jacket and chrome chain-link belt and black jeans. Dillon's clothes were a little big for me, but I'd grow into them.

I sat there.

The phone rang and Pen answered. It was Detective Mohatt, and I could hear him across the room. "We got them."

"Where were they? Up in the rocks?"

"Packing their bags. Getting ready to clear out."

"They give you trouble?"

"Some. No injuries."

"Are they talking?"

"Talking my ear off. Each trying to say the other ones did it. Give them enough rope, they'll hang themselves. Tell Shawn I said be tough. We got them."

After Pen hung up, he looked at me, and I just nodded at him. He understood and didn't try to say anything. He knew it wasn't like an answer.

That was a long evening. I didn't feel like watching TV. I wanted to call Monica, but I felt like I ought to hold off. Penn tried to play me a game of rummy, but I couldn't concentrate. I didn't know whether I ought to go to school in the morning or not. Nothing felt right.

I went to bed on the sofa when it was time, but I didn't sleep. I lay there for hours, bone tired, but I couldn't seem to get settled or feel finished with the day. The day I buried my brother.

Dillon was dead.

Dillon, or that thing that used to be Dillon—it was out there lying in the ground.

The hollow feeling in my chest lifted me up off the couch, finally. I pulled on my jeans and shirt and shoes. Could hear Pen snoring—I liked the way he snored, quiet and smooth, like a new V-12. I didn't wake him, but I left him a note on the table: *I'll be back soon. Do Not Worry. Tuff.*

I took the car keys and drove myself up to the Gardens at four in the morning.

The moon was nearly full and smack overhead in the dome of the sky, like a ceiling fixture. It wasn't hard to walk across the lawns and find Dillon's grave.

I guess I was kind of dazed from being up so late. At first, in the moonlight, I thought I saw a fluffy quilt over Dillon. Then I saw what it was: they had heaped all the funeral flowers

116

on top of the mound. And there was a bench sitting beside it for people like me. After a while they would take the bench away, and then I was supposed to forget about my brother except maybe once a year on Memorial Day.

I would never forget him.

I sat on the goddamn bench. Cried a little. Not too bad. Being out in the night with Dillon helped me feel better. There were trees, and the moon shining down with a big hazy halo around it, and wind in my hair. Always wind on those hills by the river. I could see the water shining down below, a mile wide. It wasn't a bad place for Dillon to be, lying under all them stars.

Dillon, about ten years old, when I'm about eight, and we have walked all the way to Quarryville to see some dumb magician at the fire hall, but they won't let us in because we don't have an adult with us—that's what they say. The real reason is because we're dirty and ragged and the wrong sort. I want so bad to see that stupid magician. I've always kind of believed in magic, like if I knew the secret I could

pull a father or something out of a hat, I
could be somebody else.

   Anyway, they shut the doors in our
faces, and I'm mad and sad enough to cry.
I don't cry, of course, because I am Tuff. I
don't say anything, but Dillon knows how
I feel.

   "C'mon," he says, and he leads me down
to the riverbank. We just sit there. It is
dusk. All along the banks, the fireflies are
drifting up from the grass like lighted
bubbles, and out in the channel the fish
are jumping. A big gray heron flies over
like something prehistoric. The peace seeps
into me.

   Dillon says, "Tuff, don't feel bad. We got
things they don't."

   "Sure," I say, not believing him.

Yet years later there I sat, remembering
what we had. What I still had.

I whispered, "Dillon, this is dumb. I know
you can't hear me or anything. But I kind of
believe in you. I kind of believe in you
and me."

I kind of believed in the river. I could go
down and sit by all that water, and in a weird
way Dillon would be there for me. In me. Life

was hard, it cut like a knife, yet some things it could not cut away. I could go off someplace, but the river would stay.

I said, "Dillon, there's this girl I really like, Monica. And there's my new pa, who is really something."

The river would stay. The river would go on flowing.

Little by little the water started to shine a clear peach color as daybreak came. Across the river the sky got silky bright. I sat watching the sun come up. The light touched the hilltops first. It found me.

I never heard a car door or footsteps, but all of a sudden my father was there, sitting down beside me.

"Pen," I said, not really surprised that he knew where I was or that he found a way to get there.

He put an arm around me, and I rested my head against him, but I didn't close my eyes. I looked at the sunrise, the sky, the shining water of the river. Peace seeped into me.

"C'mon," Pen whispered after a while. He got up, lifting me with him. "Let's get you home."

I nodded and turned to go. "Bye, Dillon," I said to the grave.